Sweet Like C
Boy

By
Tristan Fynn-Aiduenu

Sweet Like Chocolate Boy first published by Lulu Press in Great Britain as a paperback original in 2018 by Tristan Fynn-Aiduenu

Sweet Like Chocolate Boy copyright © 2018 Tristan Fynn-Aiduenu

Illustrations copyright © 2018 Dan 'Old B' Christie

Tristan Fynn-Aiduenu has asserted his right to be identified as author of this work

Cover Image: by Rob "Sloetry" Covell

Cover Design: Tristan Fynn-Aiduenu

Printed in

ISBN: 978-0-244-12782-4

A CIP Catalogue Record for this book is available at the British Library

ACKNOWLEDGMENTS

- God/Allah/Jehovah Jireh/ Nyame
- My mother, Cynthia Yankey , & My father Albert Fynn-Aiduenu
- My sister Tamsyn, my light
- All My Aunties & Uncles & My bright 'n' brilliant cousins Philan, Davina, Junior, Philip, Ameraye, Sidney
- Emmanuel Nwosu, you are just....*supernova happens*
- The ridiculously talented artist Danny Christie AKA OLD B
- All my friends. You know who you are. Don't want no one to get jel if I forget to write your name coz I'm doing this at 4am in the morning and I'm currently living on Freeway Cola from Lidl
- All past, present and future casts & crews of SLCB
- Toby Clarke, Marc Benga, Tejiri Obano, Aaron J Gordon, Lynette Linton, Sean Graham, Kalungi Ssbendeke, Conrad Kira, John Gordon – the flavouring SLCB needed
- The vitality of the children from Hendon School and my old peers in Westminster City School
- The game changing collective: The Initiative.dkf
- The support of companies: Dreamarts Youth Charity, Alwayz Kreative, Playback Drama
- All previous, present and future venues
- Graham White and all at Roehampton University
- The Royal Central School of Speech & Drama
- Stockwell
- Satan for thinking he got me down
- You

CAST

Bernard Mensah as MARS/JAMES/PROPHET/BOUNTY's DAD/BOY

Previous credits include:

12 Angry People (East 15), The Nativity (BBC Films), Young Simba (Lion King, Disney)

Michael Levi Fatogun as BOUNTY/ GHOST/FANTASIA's DAD/ GUY/PM

Previous credits include:

Doctors (BBC), Emmerdale (ITV) , Safe (London Theatre Workshop), Sublime (Tristan Bates Theatre)

Jade Hackett as FANTASIA/SIA/SANDRA/MICHELE/ NURSE

Previous credits include:

The Tide (Talawa), Nine Night (National Theatre/Trafalgar Studios), Sylvia (Old Vic)

Alice Fofana as GOD

Previous credits include:

Peckham Soap Opera (Royal Court), Common (National Theatre), Lessons in Love and Violence (Royal Opera House)

CREW

Tristan Fynn-Aiduenu as DIRECTOR/WRITER

Tristan Fynn-Aiduenu's recent credits include writing & producing SKEEN! and Black Attack (Bush Theatre); and Timbuktu by award-winning company Nouveau Riche (Theatre Royal Stratford East); assistant directing The Brothers' Size (Young Vic), Little Baby Jesus (Orange Tree Theatre). He is the 2019 JMK Award Winning Director and was nominated for Most Promising Playwright from the 2018 Offies

Emmanuel Nwosu as CO-PRODUCER

Emmanuel is a producer of theatre, poetry and youth arts activities. He has produced the 2018 production and tour of sold out stage play Ile La Wa by poet Tolu Ageblusi, independent theatre company East London Shakespeare and is project manager/founding member for award winning CIC Alwayz Kreative.

Tara Usher as SET & COSTUME DESIGNER

Shadé Joseph as SOUND DESIGNER

Sean Graham as MOVEMENT DIRECTOR

Alice Fofana as ASSISTANT DIRECTOR

Bethany Gupwell as LIGHTING DESIGNER

Venues

This playtext was produced to coincide with the 2019 UK tour at the following venues:

- The Battersea Arts Centre, London – 25th-29th June

- Tobacco Factory Theatres, Bristol – 3rd-6th July

- Studio 3 Arts, Essex – 13th-14th July

- Theatre Peckham, London – 20th July

- The Lowry, Salford – 7th September

Previous Productions

This play performed professionally at The Jack Studio Theatre in Brockley, London in Oct 2018 for 3 weeks. The production was co-produced by Initiative.dkf with the following cast

Andrew Umerah as MARS/JAMES /PROPHET/BOUNTY's DAD/BOY

Michael Levi Fatogun as BOUNTY/GHOST.P/FANTASIA's DAD/ GUY/PM

Veronica Beatrice Lewis as FANTASIA/SIA/SANDRA/MICHELLE/ NURSE

Alice Fofana as GOD

The Play

Key

▬ = **Double dash line after a word of speech** = Indicates an interruption

BUT

▬ = **Double dash line with no words either side** = active silence (it is at the discretion of the director to do whatever is natural in these silences)

[ ] = **square brackets**= words said in closed brackets are meant to be spoken , but the intention must be felt in the silence or physicalized.

/ = **Forward slash** = when two or more characters talk over each other.

~ = **Tilde** = A string of thoughts developing through description, momentum and intensity. ACTORS NOTE: The way this can be physicalized in rehearsal is to pat your chest every time you reach tilde whilst speaking and immediately bounce of the energy it gives you.

CHARACTERS

MARS

BOUNTY

BOUNTY's DAD (B.DAD)

SANDRA a.k.a The GIRL

MICHELLE

SIA, real and FANTASIA, the apparition

FANTASIA'S DAD (F.DAD)

JAMES

POLICEMAN(PM)

PROPHET, alive, & GHOST PROPHET (GHOST),the dead

GUY

BOY

SKINHEAD

NURSE

GOD The DJ

SETTING

An unnamed town in the mythical London Borough of Obsidian.

Then and Now.

AUTHOR's NOTE:

The piece can be performed of a cast size from the minimum of 3 (by making GOD a voiceover) and the maximum of 13. This is at the director's discretion. Apart from James, Nurse, Policeman and Fantasia's dad (who are white) – all other characters must be played by Black or Black Mixed Heritage actors. Please honour the punctuation (and sometimes lack of it). This piece is alive when Garage, Grime and Jungle music pumps through it.

This text was sent to press before rehearsals started.

For Ishmail Bangura

PROLOGUE/ALPHA

A

As audience enter... GOD (The DJ) welcomes them to the blinding tale via a mega music mix of Garage, Jungle & Grime. Then we hear the epic...

GOD: YO! (awaiting response) MANNA SAID YOOOOOO! Is that how you greet your maker?

How we feeling family? (awaiting responses. Responds)

Well, I got a tale for you. Two. Two times, Two lines, two boys ~ skanking on the groove this beautiful black disc of life ~ and we gonna be continually switching from the A to the B Side ~ and during the ride ~ I beg you analyse what you find from the 80s, 90s ~ all the way to the present tide that our children and great grandchildren may need to presently swim through. Ya si mi?

But first, we're gonna affi start at the end ~ how the devil wants. So let us get INSSSIIIDE

We are dropped into Limbo

The sounds of a river. A man is floating. His eyes are closed. He has drowned.

GOD: How the obroni make a chocolate bar from scraaaaaaaaaaaaaaatch.

GOD spins on her decks As the woman speaks, the DJ commands the waves with her turntables, creating a step garage beat. The wave toss and turn the floating man and eventually wakes him up.

The waves almost fall in line with exactly what the voice over describes.

First, they will heat water in a medium sized saucepan. They'll let it simmer, with promises of safety and inclusion.

Second, they will retrieve your cocoa beans and grind them into fine powder. A shadow of their former unified, rock-hard selves. Easier to manage, dears.

They will sweeten the mess with refined sugar and then cream together a pound of butter, buttering them up. Becoming a paste. The raw consistency is rancid and who can indulge in rancid chocolate?

Bring to boil and watch it bubble and toil.

But one must then cool it down and pour it into bowl. They can't want an explosion on their hands, now can they?

Pour in the milk from the promised land.

And then let it refrigerate.

Freeze it in time.

The man is spurted out into our world, he seems dead...

The man gasps as he catches air.

He takes a moment, then looks at his hands, body and then surroundings in complete confusion.

BOUNTY: Bounty's back... Bounty's... BBB-Bounty's

Why can't Bounty say-

GOD: I?

BOUNTY: Who are you?

> *BOUNTY notices where he is.*

Antebellum Bridge. Bounty doesn't understand. Bounty jumped. Bounty felt the water fill him

> *The sound of chains fastening onto BOUNTY, he is shackled.*

AHHHHHHHH!

> *He can feel the energy rising in him and – like a wave of boiling water – BOUNTY is blowing backward.*

> *GOD sends in the GIRL...*

> *She is an ethereal being draped in a spiritual blue. She swoops down. She sees BOUNTY is in pain. BOUNTY is scared of her at first. Then realises who she is. He is mortified. She tells him to shhh.*

GIRL: You best shut up and go back Bounty... or there will be much worse...

How far back?

> *The DJ spins music to communicate: 'Start from 1986'.*

> *The GIRL begins to mould the power in her hands.*

Right dickhead, I'mma make this quick. I ain't gonna let you go under ~ You ain't gonna recognize us, *(indicates Audience)* but we're always there ~ BUT You ended your story and you and I both know it ain't complete ~ You have your whole life , today, to repair what needs filling or there ain't much more I can do for you.

The DJ casts a light with her sounds. We hear the beginning of 'Sweet Like Chocolate, Boy' by Shanks and Bigfoot.

BOUNTY sees a figure that we cannot in the light, he recognizes it.

BOUNTY: Is that... [him]?

GIRL: He cannot move properly till you finish it.

BOUNTY: WHY ARE YOU DOING THIS? JUST LET ME DIE.

The boiling water sears his skin. BOUNTY looks to GOD.

GIRL: Yeah you best be raising your voice to your maker like that. Okay okay okay, I think I got it!

The GIRL finishes manifesting the power in her hand. She grabs BOUNTY's head and locks onto a scar underneath his eye. She shows the scar to GOD

This scar big enough?

GOD nods.

Okay...

The power in her hand is formed.

Bounty, remember what I always say – 'Those that cannot hear...

BOUNTY: ...must feel'??

The GIRL slams the power into BOUNTY's scar and it sends him hurtling back through time.

GIRL: Two stories. Two Lines. Intertwined. Hurry Bounty, the chocolate is melting ~ and from up here... we can smell the burn.

ONE

1. MARS

MARS: BBUUUUUUUUUUUUYYYAAAKKKKAASHAAA!

11:59am.

Try breaking the wakeup/getup sleep barrier just like so.
Like you are calling out to Gods and the day belongs only
to you. You will have enough energy to:

Go school, duss dyslexia and dry teachers, cook some
banging jerk, charge 10 downing street, slay the system,
demolish dragons, tell Tanisha about herself, come like
Neo and stop bullets, wash the world, move mountains,
win the girl and from that Miss feel true loves kiss – as
long as she has no tree bark-lip. Get Cocoa butter
Vaseline on that ish pronto.

And as my super sexy (cos you know I'm sexy innit,
don't lie) my super sexy self is basking in this super mega
HD, Mario kart morning sun,

With everything looking slyly sharper than usual- like
the sun's rays are a knife.

The dead are gully-creeping into the day.

Don't watch that.

              Starts to get dressed.

Call me Mars.

I'm a walking, talking madting.

Da dreamer, da intergalactic piece of nougat goodness
that is actually – Out of Twix, Yorkie, Snickers, err…

Yorkie raisin and nut... is the lightest of them all like calorie-wise. So please ladies.

Take a bite.

12.15! Okay okay.

Today is a day. Of movement. Of me moving forward

Don't expect no gangland, bang bang history round 'ere. No backtracking.

Jollof breakfast because Cornflakes and that bull don't do nothing to satisfy the morning hunger.

Hmm, no salt and done with easy cook rice. This is pagan.

Mum!

--

Mum!

--

Mummy!

Gone to work early probably. Yeah. Get ready to set –

> *Doorbell rings. MARS is scared. The doorbell rings again.*

Hol' one second.

> *After a breath, MARS opens the door.*

NURSE: Everything alright Moses?

MARS: Yep yep.

NURSE: Ready for your lovely stroll today.

MARS: Yep yep.

NURSE: Right so this is the first time you're on a community
           treatment order cos you been such a good boy ~ haven't
           you been a good boy? ~ am I right?

MARS: Yeah I guess but –

NURSE: So just some quick things –

> *Tone dramatically changes to dark. Whilst she
> talks she administers MARS' medication and
> escorts him outside.*

           You are under section 3 of the Mental Health Act ~
           Which means you are a danger to yourself or the public ~
           I have the right to treat you without your consent ~ I am
           the key holder to your freedom ~ you meet the conditions
           we have set out for you ~ or we will never ever let you go
           ~ like meeting me for your first appointment at 3pm ~
           and here you are!

MARS: *(To Audience)* Outside... *(To NURSE)* I... Erm –

NURSE: Anything the matter Moses?

           You know you can't miss this first appointment. Or
           we're gonna have to put you back in hos-

MARS: Nah! Course, course. I'll be there.

NURSE: Alright love, you take care of yourself now.

> *NURSE leaves.*

MARS: Wow... 12.30. Wow! It's set. I'm ready. I'm ready.

           Mental playlist of bangers set!

           There is a woman ~ a princess ~ In a 4 bedroom prison ~
           in a place only known as Elysium Gardens ~ all the way
           on the other side of the borough ~ And she is calling for
           her knight.

           Me, obviously.

To infinity and beyond the high rise flat.

2. BOUNTY

BOUNTY: Bounty was a child brought into the world in 80s Black Britain.

A decade brimming red with the fire and the funk in the furnace of black power. Nobody skinteet with the Babylon. People marching and moving themselves for what they think is right. An ebony justice.

Reggae, Marley, kente, comedy, The Real McCoy, Desmonds, Buffalo soldiers, Dreadlock rastas. Jerk Chicken, Fufu.

Not Foh foh. FUFU.

Cultural explosions on a borough wide scale.

All quite exciting times really. At least, they would've been… if you weren't Bounty. Bounty lived in a very nice house, in a very nice street, in a very quiet area, in a very loud borough called Obsidian.

Bounty had a very constant father and a very calm… quiet, now pre-deceased mother.

JAMES: Oi monkey head! Stop staring into space and hurry you up na mon. We're gonna be late for school!

BOUNTY: 1986. Bounty was 7 and James Torbright has finally called Bounty a monkey. He'd been watching *Love Thy Neighbour*. James Torbright… was not very bright. Bless him though he was so racist that…

He didn't mean it though; you could tell by the pool of baby blue innocence that swam in his eye.

He was the only real friend Bounty had. Convinced Bounty not to bleach himself with Jif because then he wouldn't be able to cook spicy plantain no more.

(To JAMES) Come on then you... white rhino?

JAMES: Yeah. rhino. Like that. Oh yeah, I bought your 'cousin' a doll. I couldn't find any really sexy black Barbies so I just bought her a gollywog. It's fluffy and quite frightening to ME but it's black so she can feel good about herself.

BOUNTY: *(To Audience)* Bless him... Please.

3. MARS

MARS: *(To Audience)* To get to where I need to Elysium Gardens, I gotta go over Antebellum Bridge. The ivory bone-marrow-walkway 'tween the rich and the poor. Rub against it the wrong way and you shall hear the shackles of time. That's where our damsel in the distress says she is drowning in. Now it's a little hard for me – crossing that bridge I mean. It's cos that's where my-

Drop is heard.

Backtracking. Nope! Anyway...

Notices around him.

You ever walked out of your estate and felt there's something beautiful here, but nobody is happy enough to see it?

Like, in midsummer, when the 3pm lights just hits the oversized Lambeth council windows and I swear you feel like you walking in Oz cos the estate looks like it's made from pure gold. And it ain't fool's gold either. It's the gold that you only get to truly see when you're on your ones.

Or when it's spring, and everything is so technicoloured that you feel like if you a remove a brick ~ you're gonna get licked by a bright, coloured ray of light. Like the whole estate is some pressurized Febreze spray can and we're all just cooped up in it, waiting to explode and constantly we're getting pricked by pricks who wanna see how much they can test us. But the aura, the smell inside the can is so strong, so passionate, so real and so, so, SO much potential and you can smell all the different countries just crammed into one and I can smell it and I can feel it…

And I know it's there

I know it's there

I know it's there.

But… nobody else wants to admit it

Chaa…

Well, as a soldier in an ever-combusting London Borough of Obsidian, I guess it's up to me to change that… That's what my girl says anyway.

A Xena who slays knights and dragons with the whip of her REAL hair. She has the world in her eyes,

The universe in her thighs,

Heaven on her tongue and

HELL in her bum.

Fantasia Johnson. So we gotta go through –

1.30pm

Policeman. Dickhead in suit. Passing me giving me the atheistic, cold eye.

PM: You're alright son?

MARS: Oooh he playing dirty. 'I ain't…'

Wait, she said they'd do this. He looking for a reaction, looking deep for a reaction right?

'I'm fine thank you... Pops'

PM: I am not your father. Learn some manners son.

MARS: The hypocrisy. Some any Tesco brand of policeman.

PM: *(Quietly)* Whatchu smiling about?

MARS: Nothing.

PM: Why do I find it hard to believe you?

MARS: Nuffin that concerns you and your duty you killing breddas in the street. *(To Audience)* She taught me that one.

PM: Don't you dare, you —

MARS :   You what? Say it. Shame the devil.

PM: You know nothing...

MARS: *(To Audience)* And with his stone heavy heart, he is on his way.

Can't ruin my day today.

Can't make me feel low.

Nah.

No.

Bout Son ~ you ain't nuffin ~ and by the end of today you ain't gonna learn you can't kill us ~ you can't /clamp us ~

The sound of running water.

YOU CAN'T clamp me–

The water scares MARS.

It's happening again...

The water fills the MARS' veins. He takes a deep breath.

Fantasia, Fantasia, Fantasia, Fantasia, Fantasia

The water subsides. FANTASIA appears as a vision.

FANTASIA: Mars, don't get distracted ~ we got an event to be enacted~

Come rain or shine ~ and let our souls combine and watch as we make galaxies align ~ malfunction the system design~ whilst making love to old-school grime ~ cos you so fiiiine.

You're gonna see me at 3.30 today right?

MARS nods.

Then forget the babylon ~ let's stain the white

we got bigger battles to fight ~My star-crossed knight.

Blows him a kiss.

MARS: This is why I done called on you lot. Every time I

backtrack... But obviously I can't be chirpsing up her name like that, calming down demons when man's tryna do the ting innit? So don't let me backtrack yeah?

2pm?! Shit, she'll trash me if I'm late

Forward we go fam!

4. BOUNTY

BOUNTY: 1990. 11 years old.

                 Just at the side of Aggro Estate . Bounty was on the way
                 back from delivering some food to his dad. And, it was in
                 the corner of Aggro Estate, D Block...

                 Bounty witnessed female genitalia for the very first time.

                 In all its wet, urinating glory. A girl of the age of 12 did
                 a Michael Johnson across 3 lanes,

                 had her dress by her ankles by the 2nd lane,

                 squat firmly in the groove of this jungle

                 and from her loins gushed the furious beer coloured rivers
                 of she, watering the cracks in the pavement for all to see.

                      Song 'Back to Life' by Soul II Soul plays. GIRL
                      tries to sing along as it plays in her Walkman.
                      The singing is slightly off beat and out of tempo.
                      Also, she is attempting to aim her pee.

BOUNTY: Being in a strict household where things are kept hush
                 hush so to speak, watching a vagina do what it do live
                 was quite a sight to behold. This orifice,

                 this gently layered,

                 soft,

                 fragile,

                 pink as the sky is blue,

                 Sacred as the morning dew

                 Hole...

SANDRA: *(To BOUNTY)* Whhhhyyyyy ya lookin at meee?

BOUNTY: *(To Audience)* Bounty caught himself unfolding the
                 female form when he realized exactly who he was

unfolding. Sandra Banshina. A girl so heavily salted, the
wrong comment sent her way could – would – result in
hypertension ~ Drain the ocean bed and you shall find her
cussing hyperventilating fish at the bottom of the big blue
sea, chilling on tectonic plates and fingering fault lines-

SANDRA: Oi... BOUNTY. You're propa indecent yanna, tryna
            check me out when I'm having a private piss—

BOUNTY: In the middle of the estate Sandra...

SANDRA: Weeeellllll, if you LIVED on this estate you would
            knoooow that ain't nobody ever comes here unless they
            wanna finalize a drug deal and the po-po get a cut of the
            crop too so they make this their blind spot
            aaannnnnyyywayyyyyyyy. Ma brother told me, star.

BOUNTY: I see. Okay, let me leave you to i—

SANDRA: BUT DID I SAY YOU CAN LEAVE? Come like ya
            gentleman but ya ready to duss and leave a damsel on her
            onesome wid 'er punani dripping. Typical blackman. You
            disgust me. Sooooo BACK TO DI QUESTION.
            Whhhyyyy yaa looking at me? You act like you never
            seen a pum-pum before.

BOUNTY: A what?

SANDRA: A pum-pum. *(Points to her genitalia)*

BOUNTY: Oh. YEAAAH! Course I have!

SANDRA: Really, when?

BOUNTY: Well um...I...

SANDRA: *(Hugh gasp)* YOU NEVER SEEN PUM PUM BEFORE?
            Whaaaat! I'mma have to teach about life bredrin.

            These flaps right 'ere are...

            Like...

the beginnings of civilization my yute. Like kingdoms n stuff innit. You 'affi know this ish pronto. That's what ma mum says anyway ~ She and Aunty Tante tell me though that white men and oreos ~ like YOOOOU ~ put black gyal – who have the best pum-pum might I just include – into stereotypes and stop them from ruling the world. Blooooodclarrrt. You can either be a mammy or a sketel ~ Tante said I should choose neither but enjoy the benefits of both ~ Ya hear mi Bounty?

BOUNTY: Yes yes but isn't that slightly [promiscuous] –

SANDRA: BUT H'IMAGINE, Lissen Lissen two days after that I had to box up Lisa Stafford – y'know, white girl from your sides, ya si me? – cos her watless mudda cussed out Tante for preaching in da street ~ Like that dinnerlady can speak propa h'english anywaaaay ~ Before I ruined her life – you're standing in my piss

BOUNTY: Oh /my!

SANDRA: /LISSEN! – told her about what Tante was trying to preach –

BOUNTY: My dad /gonna kill –

SANDRA: bout the sketel and mammy thing. She come chat like she sweetie bout 'I think you should choose mammy. Mammies are'

KA-KONK. Did I not tump her in her lacklustre

teeth-like-piano-key

breath-committing-blasphemy

face-like-a-killing-spree-with-her-acne

DUTTY MOUT.

Did I say I was Irissshhhhh?

Pause.

BOUNTY: *(To Audience)* Do your feel your blood pressure rising

already?

(To Sandra) Yes. Alright, your 'pum-pum' ain't expose
no more so I have to be on my way—

SANDRA: Kiss me.

BOUNTY: I beg your pardon?

SANDRA: You heard me. I want you to kiss me. Like proper deep
'n' that. Proper Black Man kiss where they smother the
face and that.

BOUNTY: W-why?

SANDRA: Coz I chose exposed mi self for your crusty rass and
beautiful tings like ma coochie ain't for any man and they
must be exciting that little Iceland sausage. Plus ya can't
be a proper bredrin if ya can't kiss a woman correct, ya si
mi? And... and...

BOUNTY: But Sandra I don't...

SANDRA: Then ya 'affi learn. If you don't I'll knooooock you into
next weeek.

BOUNTY: Okay.

SANDRA: Good.

BOUNTY: Just don't hit me too hard okay?

SANDRA: WHAT?

*SANDRA pulls BOUNTY towards her and kisses
him. It's a bit of struggle between the two but
then they both ease up and allow the moment to
happen. Then Sandra steps back savouring the
taste.*

BOUNTY: *(To Audience)* Her kiss tasted like... Bacon. Like when
you have left bacon in the oven for too long and it is

popping away with all its lard and smoke and salt ~ and then you take it out of the oven and it's indelibly crispy, tanning in its own juices and you lick it and it's like 'ooooooh, this is fattening'.

SANDRA: Your kiss is ...sweet. Tryna give mi diabetes, which ain't ma cup of cocoa. Been bumlicking the Babylon for too long so I can taste their additives to eeeeverything. It's sad...

One day you'll forget us ~ You'll forget me. ~You'll forget we were even there.

BUUUUUT,

Sandra, peers into BOUNTY's bag and eats some of his food.

We're gonna woooork on it. Ya understand. Those that cannot hear, must feel.

SANDRA exits

BOUNTY: *(To Audience)* She didn't even wash her hands.

5. MARS

MARS: There she is!

I'm standing outside the ramshackle bookies with men gone past their sell-by-date and there Fantasia Johnson is, right in the corner on some backoff box TV, on Community Channel. Listen, she speaks.

SIA (The real-life version of FANTASIA) appears.

SIA: Where are you?

Who are you now?

Where are we heading to?

Are you ready to bow?

Because the massas them, they got whips.

Thinner than the eye can see.

But when it hits, it clips,

Shredding our identity.

We are on the frontline

And our soldiers are falling.

Whips, wounds and bullets

Nein! Holocaust-a-calling

Muhammed Shakur - Prophet- is dead

And it ain't no accident.

20 mortal wounds to the head

Because black blood is their sacrament.

Vampires…

But the vampire slayers are coming.

The TV intensifies and SIA turns into FANTASIA

FANTASIA: And Mars, you and I shall be running to promiseland.
So at 3.30, Promise me ~
And show me the power of a black, king's masculine
ferocity ~
March with me
Today ~
No/ Justice? ~
NO Way

Drunken GUY approaches.

GUY: Ain't no such fing as justice ~ turn /over this Oxford
        speaking thot man

        TV switches.

MARS: *(To men)* EY PUT IT BACK MAN!

        GUY approaches, looking.

GUY: OY, don't raise your voice in 'ere ,yout. They may call
        me coolie but I ain't cool, ya hear my yout? Now gimme
        a pound or piss off my yout!

MARS: What is up with everybody tinking I'm their yout?

        This bookie seems old before his time. Dusty. Got one
        dirty moulded gash at the side of his head that he
        desperately trying to with his single acre of dark 'n'
        loveless texturized mess. Almost like soot is flaring from
        it. It's powered by

        Melted promises and roaring lies ~you gambled your life
        away and left ya woman crying didn't you? ~

        Left the kids crying didn't you? ~

        All for that 40 acres and a mule ~

        That you tink Ladbrokes gonna just drop on ya lap
        right?~

        You remind me of him ~ YOU ARE WASTE

GUY: I'M GONNA CRACK YOUR SKULL LIKE YOUR
        NAME'S HUMPTY.

MARS: Is it? Is it bredrin? COME THEN!

        (To Audience) I can't fight for shit.

        (To GUY) GO SUCK YOUR MUM

(To Audience) I don't even know why I said that
(Dodging punches from GUY whilst talking) Wh
madness always gotta be happening round my a
Fantasia says people are angry. *(Catches GUY's ...*
That was lucky, *(To GUY)* It's not me that's the ene—
(GUY's breath is stinking) WOOOOOOOOOF JESUS
CHRIST. *(To Audience)* Man can't be storytelling smells
like this.

> *BANG. GUY punches MARS' face as if it's in
> slow motion.*

6. BOUNTY

BOUNTY: 20th July 1994. Isandlwana Road Barbers. 15 years old.

Bounty had a close trim to finally couture the nappyness
that is black, unwashed or treated, hair. His father was
sitting in the corner, eyes glazed in a strange yellow.
Barber shop had the usual banter that barbershop do-

B. DAD: Oh shut up that nonsense. Hey. Foolish. Everyday
'Lineker, Lineker.' The other players chale! Come to
Ghana and you shallll seeeeee it buurruuuuvvvaaasss

BOUNTY: Said Bounty's father, Nana Ato Sackey. A hulking man –
a fantastic pretender -literally farming his head. Laughing
and joking but still found time to OWWWwwwww!

B. DAD: Son, keep still

BOUNTY: Bounty looked to the side, watching a boy with such
bouncy curls unbounded.

Sipping on milkshake and concocting his rude retort.

BOY: What see them doing a hat-trick with pounded yam? Nah
mate let Comfort down the road do that gov. She gives
me errrr a LOT of comfort if ya know what I meaaannn
ey ey…

BOUNTY: His skin looks like he's made from the finest soot. Like a
glistening ash. Proper Obsidian boy.

BOY: Look at your guy's nappyness though. Bredrin, ya son na touch water?

BOUNTY: And Bounty watched how the 2 by 4 compound erupts in laughter liked caged hyenas. Laughing at him. Usual. Even his Dad.

   As a single tear was about to escape,

B. DAD: Don't cry Bounty, don't show emotion. Just laugh with him. Keep gentlemanly and laugh along.

BOUNTY: So Bounty tried to laugh along, And in the midst of all the fakeness, he just caught sight of his dad. He gave the boy one [eye]

   B. DAD gives the BOUNTY the eye. Then the ultimate screw.

   And it was as if he sucked the soul out of him and hammered him into his grave with every blink.

   Enter SANDRA

SANDRA: OI!

BOUNTY: The ever-gracious Sandra.

   The whole place froze. It's a bit like walking into the wrong toilet. A girl has violated the sanctity of this place. AND she wasn't commercially attractive! Look away Bounty before she's—

SANDRA: BOUNTY!

BOUNTY: *(Sotto)* Ugh.

SANDRA: Are you a dog? Is you Scooby doo? WHHHYY are you shaving your crown? I should kill with the scissors for acting like a coconut.

BOUNTY: My d-dad –

SANDRA: Hi Uncle.

DAD: Oh, Hello my dear!

SANDRA: *(Whispers in ear like a murderer)* Daddy can't save you
                now you coon. BUT ANYWAY, I want you to meet
                someone. Meet *myyyy* uncle.

BOUNTY: A pair of flaring joggers with a boombox to

                beat the beat of the street appeared in the doorway.

                Muhammed Shakur

                aka

                Enter PROPHET.

                Prophet.

                A man with the womp of music in every lash of black
                chocolate wrapping his 6' 5 body ~ Eyes looking like
                crystals- emeralds – embedded in a royal, velvet
                mahogany face ~ looking like he the wood cut Atlas.

PROPHET: What's brewing ma brothers? Shaving off our kings again
                are we?

                Yo. Check out this thang I'm hearing. They call it Jungle.

                SANDRA plays the music

BOUNTY: Bounty was in awe of this strange new music. It had
                evolved from the sound clashing form yesteryear and was
                very…

                Uninhibited. Ever-involving. You can't do a quiet two-
                step to it because it didn't want you to because it was
                rebellious. Free.

                Kinda like San... no she's doesn't deserve nice adjectives.

                Just like…

Soul smashing Jungle mix plays.

When Bounty first saw Prophet, it felt like you had to have this get-up-n-go, black-love-on-show kinda music in you to vibe with his black orchestral self. Bounty's soul was too busy stuck on this two year old Rick Astley tune.

'Never Gonna Give You Up' by Rick Astley starts to play and BOUNTY starts to head nod quite excessively, really feeling the beat.

(Over the music) It's got quite a beat right? Like, you could actually close your eyes and imagine a black man singing this! Does that qualify?!

The music then turn into a Jungle version of the beat.

BOUNTY:	*(Snapped back to reality by SANDRA)* Owwwwwwwww
SANDRA:	Ya like, Bounty? REAAALLYY? I thought ya people were the Beach Boys
BOUNTY:	*(To audience)* Well I woulda said The Who but…
SANDRA:	Right you're taking me clubbing tonight.
BOUNTY:	Wait what?
BOY:	OY OY BOUNTY!
BOUNTY:	Said the boys in the shop. Sandra whispered something in Prophet's ear and he swooped down on the empty barber chair.
PROPHET:	What's your name?
BOUNTY:	People call me Bounty.
PROPHET:	What as in…
BOUNTY:	Yes, the chocolate bar.

PROPHET: Oh. I was going to say 'Bountiful' myself. Are you bountiful Bounty?

BOUNTY: Erm... I dunno.

PROPHET: Okay. I see. Who told you that you were a coconut?

BOUNTY: ...Everybody.

PROPHET: You mean your black familia?

BOUNTY: No I mean... EVERYBODY... because...

I speak well and....my father speaks well...and

I live in a house instead of an estate and~ I don't really buy much Lovers Rock or Reggae as much as everyone else and~

The ladies in the Jamaican shop throw patties at me cos I don't say what I want fast enough cos there's quite a lot of choice y'know and my dad says I need to watch my carbs and I quite like Greggs and cos I like Greggs I feel fatter than the other boys who all look like shredded

I haven't got much *(whispers)* Game.

(To Audience) He laughed when Bounty said that.

(To PROPHET) I don't really know how to be black...

(To Audience) He frowned when Bounty said that.

PROPHET: Hmmm. What a miseducation. It's cool. Y'know what you need? You need a brother... fath—

B.DAD: *(Clears throat)* I think that's enough.

BOUNTY: Said Bounty's father,

PROPHET: Oh no disrespect Uncle, I was just getting to know your son better.

B.DAD: And I think that is enough. Come on Bounty, you're looking good. Time to go home.

BOUNTY: Yes dad.

       (To Audience) Bounty went to retrieve his coat only to find no one in the shop. Not even his Dad. Just him.

       As he looked out of the window, he saw what made Sandra's eyes gleam from green to red.

       A policeman, bobby on the beat, came circling around the bouncy coolie haired soot boy. He had finished his hair, looking crisp and was writing in a bookie whilst waiting for the bus.

       He was writing dub poetry ~ anger and atrocities of Brixton 1981 and Tottenham 1985 and Stephen Lawrence only a year ago. Police man had been spat the spite of the Caribbean's so long that when he was crossing the back of the bus stop and was eavesdropping through the glass, he could understand the lingo. Especially the words, written in big bold red letters…

          The word 'MURDERER' is sung from the song
          of the same name by Barrington Levy.

       The policeman started to ask questions, of which Soot-boy was not fond of. The young man tried to leave but the policeman wouldn't let him. Asking questions and sneering UN-PC abuse. Just buying his time for his team mate to arrive. You cannot do SUS without another officer present. The Barbershop men came down to defend but the young man was compliant and told them not to worry. He knew there was nothing they could find on him. It shocked the police. So as they ran the inside of his legs, the officer with the pale white shell of a face took the opportunity to check just at the curve of the pelvis ~ just across the pubic area ~ just behind the scrotum and, just to make sure of no ill will, he DUG his nails into his testicles.

The man screamed and pushed the police officer off him, yelling 'chi chi mon' ~ By the time ghost white police officer hit the ground, the red face one already had his baton at the go and went to town

> *Watches as BOY is beaten mercilessly*
> *by the police.*

In broad daylight?

Barbershop men tried to pull the policeman off, only to find the man shivering in his own blood. "Where's Dad", Bounty thought?

From the pavement, Bounty saw the other men hurl themselves at their pig-faced enemy ~ The ghost faced one was still on his back calling back up ~ A van full of policemen poured into the streets ~ Riot shields and shining batons ~ helmets as if going to fight that dragon the tried to kill St George ~ only that the Damsel in distress was a wrathful keeper-of-the-peace ~ A black, ebony vanguard on one side ~ the men in blue on the other.

And Bounty could've been there with them. Maybe if he had even just spat... or something. But everything was so...[scary]

Then...

The entire world became grayscale. Black, White & Grey ~ Contrast at 75 % ~ Brightness 60%.

No noise. Only chaos.

And suddenly a man, police man but with no helmet~ with no hair on head or face ~ appeared in front of him. Baton ready at the go to beat Bounty's brains in. A-and Bounty was scared that he was going to die so he tried to scream but all that would crawl out was

'Please. Please don't kill me'.

And the man's eyes gleamed at this – this *dirty* submission.

And his white skin started to shine. And his red eyes became concentrated like that of a snake,

And all that crawled out of his jaws was…

SKINHEAD: Beg.

BOUNTY: And… so… Bounty put his hands up and… and got on his knees and… then he said.

SKINHEAD: Bow.

BOUNTY: So, with his hands still up, warm piss running down the side of his leg… and vision impaired…

he slowly bent down…like a slave.

And,

suddenly there was a flash… and, and the click of a camera. And the world was back to its summer colours. But smoking… And the black vanguard was watching Bounty.

Bounty… and… the body of the skinhead policeman on the floor.

Bounty ~ and the body ~ and the severed head ~ of the skinhead policeman~ 5 millimetres away.

Bounty ~ and the body ~ and the severed head ~ of the skinhead policeman ~ 5 millimetres away and his father… with his car keys in one hand and the machete from the butchers shop next door covered in human blood in the other.

Eyes on his son who he had spent a lifetime building for, only to see him bow to his captors. Sure he was disgusted. I would be.

> *Notices he could say I and is shocked , but before he can ask further questions - The waves of Limbo rise like a tidal wave and drag him away*

TWO

GOD: Gabriel! Play!

> *A short interlude as we move through time to "Gabriel -Live Garage Remix" by Roy Davis ft Peven*

1. BOUNTY

> *BOUNTY is washed up into a prison visiting room. He's sees a figure shrouded in sorrow in front of him. It is his DAD.*

BOUNTY: Oh no.

Please. Please not this. Just let him go please.

> *The chains rattle and hoists him up to the seat.*

1994. Obsidian Prison,

Bounty's dad was...

There were crusty cracks where bloodstrained veins should be. He looked ...masticated ~ No.

Derelict.

Let Bounty go to another time... please?

Bounty has learned his lesson! Mess up once and world will crumble beneath your feet. Everything stems from here. His story starts and ends here-

> *B.DAD finally notices BOUNTY with glee.*

B.DAD: Son!

BOUNTY: Daddy?

> *Silence.*

> *BOUNTY – reluctantly – sits. They take each other in.*

> *Silence.*

41

How...

How... are you?

B.DAD: -

BOUNTY: Daddy? Why did you kill that policeman?

Pause.

B.DAD: – how are you?

BOUNTY: Daddy I... I just wanna know why you killed –

B.DAD: A-and how's school/is school okay and your grades –

BOUNTY: /Daddy p-please I have got much time to talk now –

B.DAD: SON! *(Notices the room)* ...My son. There are some things you won't...I don't want you to understand.

The prison buzzer rings.

Bounty, I have to go now but/ maybe next/ time okay.

BOUNTY: You have to go? / No, no! Because of you Bonuty's fading into the walls ~Because of you I am going into care ~ and all these people just come and run into this house ~ and this is the last time I'm gonna get to see you because after this... You know – that you did what you did because of me. Right?

Right?

Beat.

B.DAD: It's good to see you.

DAD walks away.

BOUNTY: Wait. WAIT! Dad! Don't you have anything to say?

Oh... Bounty never said that. Oh.

Bounty never saw him again.

1. MARS

MARS: 2pm… or 2pm-ish

But obviously I can't know for certain cos I can't reach my phone ~ cos I'm criminally cuffed at the back of a police van! I ain't gonna describe it, ain't in the mood.

It's grey.

Phone buzzes.

Of course my phone would ring when I can't answer it. I reaalllllyyy ain't got time fi this.

Tries to wriggle to get phone out of pocket whilst talking.

It's probs Fantasia –

These cuffs feel tight. I guess this is… exciting… the panther life and dah… I think… getting arrested.

Well actually they can't arrest me cos I didn't actually do anything. Drunk guy swung for me and naturally I-I had to reciprocate the gesture innit? I told you fam, I'mma real one.

The way he cowered when I just lightly brushed the gashed on his head like. Like I was a demon. That didn't feel great. Why?

Enter POLICEMAN.

Speaking of demons – remember policeman that try chat to me earlier? Guess who got the lovely call to capture the IC3's outside the bookies.

Y'know… he kinda looks scarier from this angle. Like a levitating tombstone.

PM: Right son…

MARS: *(To Audience)* This gguyyyyyy…

PM: So full name please?

MARS:	Na you don't need that? What you gonna use it for?
PM:	You're are being given a –
MARS:	You can't arrest me! You can't arrest me!
PM:	I-I'm not here to –
MARS:	Touch me, touch me and I swear fam, I will report your arse so fast.
PM:	I'mma have to if you keep on piping up. Calm down. What is your name?
MARS:	Urmumizagoat
PM:	*(writing)* Urrr... Mumiz a... Don't tell me, Ugandan spiritual name right? Good ain't I?

Phone keeps buzzing.

MARS:	Is this your first day or suttin?
PM:	As a matter of fact *(realizes his mistake)*...that's none of your business.
MARS:	Can you at least get my phone? Please.
PM:	That how you finish speaking to a senior member of authority? Please what?
MARS:	Please...sir.
PM:	Now that's what I like. A little bit-a respect lad. /Now I can help you out. Ah a Nokia 3310. I remember these from way back lad. Bit old school for you!
MARS:	OKAY OKAY yes yes, please hurry please please/

Phone stops ringing.

AAAh missed it.

PM:	Don't worry, looks like you got 3 voicemails.

Dials voicemail. Usual phone woman speaks. Then:

VOICE: Message from 07–

                The girl appears as FANTASIA.

FANTASIA: Mars, remember go by the meat shop

                What we're gonna do will include a likkle chop chop

                Don't flop!

MARS: Yes baby.

VOICE: Message from 07

                The GIRL appears as NURSE.

NURSE: Hi Mars, it's Lisa Stafford here from the Obsidian centre. Just to say it is now 2:57 and we have yet to see you roll through these doors so just to remind you that ~ *(Serious tone change)* if you do not /show up you will be dumped back in the Obsidian Hospital like the wretch –

MARS: / You can skip – y-you can skip that one please sir!

VOICE: Message from 07

MARS: Mum!

                The GIRL walks on as Mars' MUM. Silence. She is solemn. She tries to speak but nothing comes out. Sorrowful, she runs away.

                Mum?

VOICE: End of messages.

MARS: *(To Audience)* Anyway, it's 2:58 probs and I need to get out of here. Let's wax lyrical the most ultimate bumlick. Sorry guys, a lotta shit coming…

                (To PM) My fair gentleman. I am sorry for the disturbance thus caused by my heinous actions and shubadabbe skina montin guoghujhsuhujlafugeil bbrgyfvbhagfafkgiufvwlgbulwn *(fart sound)*

bupalupashabbalabbadingdon mrloverman and you being the fantastic white rare rhino that you are –

PM: What did you call me? Just now… what did you call me?

MARS: Umm… a rhino… in like a good sense though. They're strong and that.

PM: Yeah… Rhino… like that. *(Looks to MARS. Unshackles his cuffs)* Go on son.

MARS: I thank very much sir for my freedom and for being the ULTIMATE DICKHEAD FAM YOU…

(To Audience) Look at him. He don't hear me like. He don't even hear when the radio start calling for an IC3 on the loose after not showing up to his 3pm appointment!

He just sat there, grinning so big it creates earthquakes and turquoise landslides in the gravel of his face and… brings out the sapphire in his eyes. Wow…

PM is laughing and crying at the same time.

Well… too bad I'mma soon have to rip them out.

MARS runs.

2. BOUNTY

BOUNTY: Things only get worse from here. There is NOTHING-

BOUNTY feels a sharp pain as the shackles of him rattles.

Fine.

JAMES appears.

JAMES: Oi, Monkey head. Ha! You turned ya head!

BOUNTY: This is …4th May 1996. Bounty was 17. Cornershop and James…

James was still Bounty's best friend. But he had... grown?
[If that's the right word].

Ever so slightly.

If you look close in his eye...you saw something freeze
the rivers.

JAMES: As I was saying... do you... do you get dreams about it?

BOUNTY: 'Bout what?

JAMES: The whole day...seeing those police officers.

BOUNTY: Sometimes.

(To Audience) All the time. *(To JAMES)* James... why do
you bother with me?

JAMES: I dunno. You're cool. Not like the other black kids.
You're kinda posh, but not like in a knobhead kinda way.
Am I supposed to hate you?

BOUNTY: I think so.

JAMES: Oh. My dad says I should. He don't like you. I would let
you live with me instead of care but he'll throw Nazi
fings in your face, the reggae music will give my sister
jungle fever and you'll hate how dry my roast chicken is.
He got my brothers joining this international front fing or
sumfink though. Me though, I wanna be a bobby.

Like those tryna stop the riots.

BOUNTY: What –

JAMES: Nooooo, not like that fucking evil one. Been finking
about it for a while now. Like

knight-like and that but, like, doing good fings and that.
So we don't hate each other cos I like when you cook
your spicy fried banana and when you make hot pepper
shitty-oh sauce that can go wiv my chips.

BOUNTY: Shito[h] James.

JAMES: Yeah that's what I said. And I'm telling cos... you're.... I wanna be something good.

And I don't want you to hate me for it. Because you my best friend and... I wanna look after you I guess. *(JAMES looks up)*

BOUNTY: Thanks James.

JAMES: Now that that's all settled, I need your help mate with that Sandra chick. Ah that girl makes my prick so happy. I wanna jook her up.

BOUNTY: James... you really don't want that.

JAMES looks in the distance. He can see someone coming, he frowns.

Don't be upset with me, I can try mention your name when she next beats me up –

JAMES: He's coming...

BOUNTY: *(To Audience)* Enter Prophet.

PROPHET: Excuse me, young man, I'd like to talk to Bounty. Can ya give us a sec?

BOUNTY: James knows what time it is and he backs away. But the two clock each other with a stare so potent it could poison the iris. Like he saw a black-

PROPHET: Bounty, walk with me. How you been?

BOUNTY: OKAY I guess.

PROPHET: How's ya new care home? I'm sorry bout your dad, Sandra told me.

BOUNTY: *(sotto)* Flipping Sandra...

PROPHET: Listen...what are you up to today? I wanna show you something.

BOUNTY: We arrived and this small, battered looking community centre.

PROPHET: This is Black Star Saturday School. Come in Bounty...

BOUNTY: The Saturday School was moderately sized in terms of pupils, but contained every shade of black and mixed race known to man. And they were all so eager to learn.

The place had a heartbeat ~ a vibration of education for the upcoming hip hop nation~ see on the wall Crayola hieroglyphics of Tutankhamun beating up a cowboy who called Mary Seacole a gyppo ~ a league of melanin proud superheroes dead, alive and those that only the black child could contrive.

PROPHET: Bounty. I'm showing this because... you have something. Something great. Gorgeous. Rough, Damaged but there. It sparkles right now Bounty but ~ with my help ~ it will illuminate. You can come live with me, live just upstairs. I-it's basic accommodation but –

BOUNTY: Prophet... I-I don't have any money to pay for all this.

PROPHET: I don't want you to pay nothing. This is ma school. This is your school. Your new home. If you want it to be. The blackness that you think you don't own. That's bull. That ain't nothing but surface level ~ distraction.

The depth of blackness tears powerfully through the earth's core and spills out into the nebula of multi-verses ~ It's the succulent sauce that has stirred the gumbo of time and flavours the palette of the Gods ~ It's what makes ya eyes glisten, ya walk jive, ya soul pop and ya love mighty ~ it is ever-changing ~ communal and individual ~ it is the paradox that you feel belies you ~ You have all this in you, and ya own special prism God has gifted you to emit it in~ You are black whether they tell you or not.

Whether you think it or not. I just want you to learn to love it man.

But of course, I'm just talking, know what I mean. You don't feel it. But come here and you will. Be with me and you will.

Do you want this Bounty?

PROPHET reaches out his hand.

BOUNTY: *(To Audience)* Bounty felt something real when he looked at Prophet's battered and bruised hands. A real worker man's hands.

> *BOUNTY goes to shake PROPHET's hand then...*

> *At the moment of touching, the DJ spins and we hear a powerful mix of Negro spirituals with jungle backing tracks, racist American chants, the news reports of Black Lives Matter marches and the lasting sprays of gunfire. It is as if the pain and power runs rife through PROPHET's body. The moment terrifies BOUNTY and after feeling too much of the pain, he lets go. At that moment, PROPHET goes in for a hug. As if nothing happened. BOUNTY melts into the hug.*

PROPHET: OKAY Bounty. Let's get to work!

> *PROPHET walks away. BOUNTY is mortified with what just happened, but before he can react – he is whisked away by the wave of time.*

3. MARS

MARS: 2:59, I bolted boy!

Iswandlwana Road.

I

pass,

the Obsidian Medical Health Centre. One colonial looking building for true. It used to be a barber's but they gave some dyslexic haircuts so they had to be shut down.

Y'know, if I go in now... if I go in now I don't have to go back to hospital. I could just go in and get my treatment and repeat. And repeat. And repeat And –

FANTASIA appears

FANTASIA: These people wanna split open a black mind

And see what problems they can find

The active mind's diagnosis

Is the protest psychosis

Truss mi, I know this

MARS: You're right!

FANTASIA: I'm ain't bad b with lumbar lordosis

Let ma twerk show thiiiiisssssssssssssss!

MARS: Okay, she don't say that bit but I love wishing she did.

FANTASIA: MARS, FOCUS!

MARS: Yeah yeah! Sorry sorry!

FANTASIA disappears.

(To Audience) I get to the butchers shop. Them lot there carving up meat like samurai. With beautiful halal slices.

Main butcher man is slack. She said they'd do this. Ain't watching where he put his tools. Bad move.

I walk in the shop. I survey. Make sure I ain't being watched. They're there chatting in their language. The machete is on the slab. Bloodied but I packed a bag so I don't get salmonella. I take it out, mould it over my hand like so – Oh people watching, people looking – hide the hand!

This machete is part of the master-plan. I need it! I edge closer to the till. Man there asking what cut I want.

The flow of water is heard.

(To Butcher) His head. No – no I mean , I'm just looking for now.

(*To Audience*) Man gives me a disappointed nod, but it's like he can see what I wanna do. He watching me like ~ He can see ~ Can he see? Shit-shit-shit. He thinks I'm a stereotype – another black boy tryna steal a knife ~ go on then ~ go on then ~ hyper-ventilate ~Fantasia Fantasia. Fantasia Fantasia is in a... hospital

Scene swiftly changes. Enter SIA.

In a hospital with me. A year ago.

Sia ~ this fantasy ~ based on the deflated bed opposite mine ~ standing right in the window of the frame ~ and looking out towards the horizon.

'What you looking at?' I ask

SIA: I dunno

MARS: She sighs.

SIA: Sometimes, I feel so... tired

            And wired

            Trying to fire

            The world around me.

            To wake and make

            This lake of heartache

            And societal pisstakes

            Dissipate.

            And sometimes it feels like I am on my own. .

            And Sometimes

            I'd just like to be....

MARS: 'Respected?' I say

SIA: Held.

MARS: She says. 'Like a goddess ?' I say.

SIA: Like a... like a woman.

                And when he was there. When Prophet was there

                I didn't have a care

                in the world

                But now he's gone ~ and now I – we – must take the
                mantle ~ come what may

                But hey... forget about me. Are you okay?

MARS: And somethings moves inside of me. My soul is
                suspended in a space and –

                SIA transforms into FANTASIA

FANTASIA: ANND if that is so, then Mars,

                take the machete

                For there to be real revolution, things are gonna have to
                get messy.

MARS: B-but I'm scared.

FANTASIA: Mars

                Take

                The machete.

MARS: Butcherman's back is turned. But if I dare –

FANTASIA: MARS

                Take

                Your

                Machete.

MARS: I clock the time. 3.03.

               MARS takes the machete. He slides down the
               wall onto the pavement in a slump.

               Nobody. Nooobody. Saw anything?

FANTASIA: Good boy.

               Now Come to Elysium, Mars, Come get me.

               MARS – as if hypnotized – walks.

4.   BOUNTY

BOUNTY: Bounty came up with the idea of the Obsidian Jukenoo
               and the whole – and I mean the WHOLE – of the
               borough – got into it.

               Ahhh they used to bring out like stools and stools on the
               cramped pavements and be selling Jerk Chicken or
               Waakye or Bofloats, Chin chin, Kelewele, Tikka Masala,
               Roti, Bhaji- BHAAAHJI, Moimoi (but nobody ever
               really bought that unless you wanted to throw it at
               someone) , Beef and Lamb Suya.

               And every girl is in facepaint and batty riders which
               makes all the mandem on the side of the cage feel a bit
               frisky and risky and take try elegantly chat up a chick
               with their NOKAYIA 3310 !!!

               And the sun always seemed to be shining on that day and
               the evening was a time for the best getdown.

                And we showed the world the sweet side of being black
               in all its texture.

               And it was in the summer of 1997 that Bounty met
               Michelle.

And she came with this new sound in headphones. Like Jungle, but slightly more sophisticated. Not tamed, just kinda… together. Mechanical. Militant. They called it Garage.

She was blue black, the darkest girl Bounty had ever seen ~ I swear to you, it felt like the entire universe was ground in her skin. Night within night.~ straight from the bean ~ Her walk was humble and her eyes were twilight ~ her voice was green and blacks ~ her heart was pure and-

MICHELLE: Hi.

BOUNTY: Hii

        Beat.

MICHELLE: Erm, My name is Michelle.

BOUNTY: Oh. err… Hi. I'm… I'm Bounty.

MICHELLE: Is that ya real name?

BOUNTY: No no no. Sorta become my name. My real name is….

        (BOUNTY examines the side of MICHELLE's head. To Audience) A scar just at the side of her head. Underneath her weave. Never noticed that before.

            BOUNTY looks at his hands.

Scars… Maybe.

            BOUNTY reaches over to touch MICHELLE's head. But then retracts.

No.

BOUNTY: You just call me Bounty.

MICHELLE: It's nice this isn't it? All this pro-black.

BOUNTY: Yeah real nice.

MICHELLE: Not really my scene to be honest but it's nice   All the stalls and that. I wish I could set one up.

BOUNTY:	Well, why don' you? Sandra set up a £2 sherbet stand at the far end. No one's gonna buy anything but it's the determination that counts I guess. What would you sell?
MICHELLE:	Well… I, actually, since you're interested and that. I'd like someone to eat my chocolate.
BOUNTY:	Oh, I-I-I, well, so fast—
MICHELLE:	Oh oh no! I mean look…

She goes into her bag and retrieves a chocolate wrapped in foil.

Silly!

BOUNTY:	Oh, right.
MICHELLE:	It's what I do. It's all I do really. You look like you're a man of good taste and just need it to taste right y'know. Taste really good like Cadbury's but without the risk of diabetes and that. Don't want anybody dying on me now do I—
BOUNTY:	I get you. I get you. Of course. Forgive my dirty mind. Erm, I see. Okay. Yeahh. Okay. Thank you. Okay. Here goes…

BOUNTY eats the chocolate, it's horrible… at first… but then

Actually

A heart searing Garage mix plays. BOUNTY and MICHELLE dance together, souls to soul, aware of the union.

(To MICHELLE) Michelle, it's…

MICHELLE:	Is it good? Really?

BOUNTY nods.

Good. The heroin gives it a really good kick I find.

BOUNTY is mortified. They look at each other and laugh.

Don't worry, it's only ganja.

BOUNTY: Can... I can take your number? ...or your pager if that's too fast.

MICHELLE: All if it is a bit fast to be honest.

BOUNTY: Oh Sorry to intrude. I'll-

MICHELLE: But I like men of action. I'll be back, will just ask my dad. Y'know how dads are.

MICHELLE exits.

BOUNTY: As she drifted off, lightning bolts struck and the black death pulsated through the carnival.

Enter SANDRA.

SANDRA: OI. BOUNTY.

BOUNTY: God WHHYY? Sandra Banshina came, she was dragging... JAMES!

SANDRA: You see your friend yeah –

BOUNTY: Oh James – *(To Audience)* He was sloshed to the core.

JAMES: *(To SANDRA)* Come on my likkle African princessah. Want your lollipop chocolate like twix ice cream a-nom-nom!

BOUNTY MY MAN!

BOUNTY: For God's sake –

SANDRA: You need to tell milkyway over here to move clear away from me and done told him that those that cannot hear must feel –

JAMES: I wannnna feeeel your big bubu lips up against mine while mi make sweet suggzy love wiv our tonnngguuesss and I jookay ya pumpum well good. Innit I said I'd jook her pum Bounty?

SANDRA: NAAAH BOUNTY. I'm not having this. See what I done told you bout hanging out with these sorta brehs. *(To all)* SEE WHAT HAPPENS WHEN YOU INVITE THESE PEOPLE THEM TO THE COOKAOUT?

BOUNTY: He wasn't invited Sandra!

JAMES: What you mean mate? Just the other day you said we should meet up more like we used to and – HERE I AM

SANDRA: He's finally realised his Blackified self and don't want you and your racist filth near him.

JAMES: WHAT? I ain't racist? I just said I wanna have sex with wiv you! Bounty tell her you're my best friend! If he's my best friend how can I be racist? Bounty tell her!

SANDRA: Bounty, what's it gonna be?

BOUNTY: James, let's talk outside the court.

JAMES: No, Bounty. Tell her I'm your friend...

Bounty?

BOUNTY: James calm down.

JAMES: I AM CALM!

SANDRA: Get rid of him Bounty.

JAMES: Bounty tell her!

SANDRA: Tell me what? He is not a slave to you and never will be.

JAMES: Bounty stop being a banana and tell her I'm not racist man.

BOUNTY: BUT YOU ARE JAMES!

...You are.

Beat.

JAMES: What?

BOUNTY: Everything you've learnt, you're whole being is racist –

JAMES: How could you say that me? How could you say that to ME?

BOUNTY: James let me speak/

JAMES: NO!

SANDRA: After all the black martial arts I done taught you are you really gonna let him step to you like that? Capoeira his arse man. Round 1, Lick 'im na!

JAMES: You wanna fight me Bounty? You siding with them now? Them that don't even like you – only like you cos you're not a dumb black guy.

BOUNTY: No –

JAMES: Fight me then. You blacks fink your so much better but everyone knows I'd floor ya easy.

BOUNTY: Stop it James.

JAMES: All cos you so desperate to get in wid them. To fuck some black pussy. I saw that darkie you were talking to.

BOUNTY: Don't call 'er that!

JAMES charges for BOUNTY. He is manic, almost fighting like a drunken master.

JAMES: Why the fuck you fink you're soooooo special. SOOOOOO different from alla us? No wonder they killa ya dad in prison ~ wasting his time wid book smart –

In a definitive blow, BOUNTY punches JAMES back. It's a surprise.

BOUNTY: Don't you ever, EVER talk about my dad.

Well ~ Maybe ~ if you spent ya time ~ educating yourself ~ and not ~ drowning ya life away…

And Bounty hit him and hit him again and hit him

And I hit him and hit him and kick him and punch him slap him and *(Mortal Kombat voice)* GET OVER HERE.

THOSE THAT CANNOT HEAR MUST FEEL.

BOUNTY unleashes a wacky, video-game like 100 hit combo with a black hadouken to finish BOY off.

(Scream of power and achievement)

HHAAAAAAAAAAAAAAAAAAAAAAAAAAAA!

Pause. JAMES looks at BOUNTY. Staggers up then runs away crying.

SANDRA: K.....O......Wow. Bounty that's what I'm [talking about]

BOUNTY: I'M SICKA YA SHIT. YOU AIN'T MA TYPE!

SANDRA runs away ugly-crying.

(To Audience) Did Bounty really say that? I guess he did.

Prophet had been watching, he just nodded and walked away. Ruined his Junkanoo. Sorry. They started it.

The crowd was shouting.

ALL: BOUNTY BOYD SANDRAA! WOOOHEEEYYY!

BOUNTY: They carried Bounty around like-like he was king. Worthwhile. The beez kneez. Yeaah. YEEEAAAAH. YEEEEEEEAAAAAAAAAAAAAHHHHH

Cheering changes when he is put in front of MICHELLE.

Michelle... I-I'm not that kinda guy –

MICHELLE: I can see that from your dinosaur punches. Dad can't. So that's my pager gone.

BOUNTY: B-but he started it!

MICHELLE: And you finished it. *(Michelle kisses BOUNTY on the cheek)* Silly.

BOUNTY: She was lovely.

Weeks passed and Bounty got to discover more and more about this girl who liked Eternal ~ adored Sweet Female Attitude ~ was avid weedhead ~ disliked the idea of people being tangoed ~ hated SMTV for making people feel 'so thiiiick, so thick so thick so thick' ~ was fascinated by this word dyslexia ~ who wanted to open up a cookery school in the estate for abused women and felt this incredible want to tear up every time she saw another black child cry.

Once again he got to see that sacred orifice that was said to have behold empires according to Sandra.

However, there was something hidden behind that glint of the night in her eye. There was something and...I've always wondered...

> *BOUNTY feels there is a power in his hand. He gives it a moment and slowly reaches over to touch MICHELLE's scar. But then...*

MICHELLE: Are you gonna leave me?

BOUNTY: Why would I leave you?

MICHELLE: I know what happens. This is what happens.

               You can go if you want. I won't hold it against you. I was a mess I know like – I just wanna live a happy life babe.

BOUNTY: No. I'm not leaving.

MICHELLE: You're not?

BOUNTY: I really like you. Like *really* like you. Past all this. Past just your looks. And you are stunning like please don't get me wrong. I feel so normal with you. And a mess and extraordinary at the same time And, dare I say it, I think you feel – or like could feel- normal and extraordinary with me. Maybe not a mess but like y'know what I mean. And if you want, I can learn to be more of a man and- /and fight and stuff and do kickboxing-

MICHELLE: /Bounty. Bounty. Bounty

That ain't you. You are you. And you… just might be…
what I been waiting for. Something solely sweet.

They share a powerful kiss that melts.

Ooookaaaaay. Can you calm your boner down now
please? My dad is coming home right about now and will
chop it off in exactly 75 seconds.

BOUNTY: *(To Audience)* Due to forgetting the use of a condom,
Bounty became a father in 1998.

And when the baby arrived... it was [beautiful]

5.   MARS

MARS: 3.20

Aggro Gardens Estate

D Block

I shouldn't be here.

LET'S TAKE A LOOK AROUND.

This

Is

A ghost estate. London's limbo where half-bred baby
mothers meander around the debris like spectres waiting
for their bullet ridden mandem to take control of their
council-flat-hold.

You know a place is damaged when the words 'hotspot'
have to be sprayed where hotspot actually is so
everybody in the estate, even the feds, know where
hotspot is.

GHOST: HEY!

MARS: Oh for …

          It's another ghost…

          So, as you probs heard me say previously we are
          marching for man who died in police custody right?

          This is him. Your new bredrin. Prophet.

          This glowing light just shining off him.

          *As GHOST speaks, MARS does his voice (the
          same voice of PROPHET)*

GHOST: Prophet knows you… your face.

          *MARS tries to leave. But the GHOST appears in
          front of him.*

GHOST: Don't move from him!

MARS: Leave me alone before I start chanting prayers bruv!

GHOST: CHANT THEM! PRAY THE MOTHERFUCKER
          AWAY.

          Pray, march, talk, organize, catalyse this bullshit

MARS: Stay AWAY from me.

          Reaches to the machete in the backpack.

GHOST: Aaah, so you armed… that's what Prophet likes to see.
          Black brothas protecting themselves.

          Fantasia may be starting the fight but we need men, we
          need men to take this shit on.

          If Prophet is a spirit then…

          Let Prophet take over your body.

MARS: What?

GHOST: Black cannot exist in its true form whilst being frozen in
          a white system.

          There is a whole hole in you. Let prophet…

MARS: NO!

GHOST: Prophet ain't gonna hurt you. Let me

> *GHOST touches MARS we hear waves mixed in
> with a garage/grime mix*

Wait... WAAAIIIIIIIT.

> *We hear the sound of MICHELLE going 'Okay
> Bounty...Okay'*

You are his...give me yo body/ AND I will never
abandon you like he did.

MARS: /No please, No stop, STOP...

> *MARS raises his Machete to strike GHOST until
> he hears the last bit of what he says...*

What?

GHOST: You think Prophet don't know? Prophet knew him.
Prophet knows. Come one, let Prophet hold you.

> *MARS, taking in the promises of something
> better, nods.*

That's ma boy. Give Prophet your hand. Give Prophet
that scar.

> *MARS, tentatively, offers his hand. GHOST
> smiles and melts into MARS's hand.*

GHOST: AHHHHHHHHHHHHHHHHHHHHHHHHHHHHHH!

> *He feels the promise in his hand.*

MARS: I feel... volcanic.

I move.

Fly

3.25.

I get to Antebellum Bridge and I..I..

> *The flowing of water. It hurts MARS but then he decides to run through it. FANTASIA & GHOST.P appear as one conjoined entity. They with a voiceover from EVERYONE.*

FANTASIA: The depth of blackness tears powerfully through the earth's core and spills out into the nebula of multi-verses ~It's the succulent sauce that has stirred the gumbo of time and flavours the palette of the Gods ~ It's what makes ya eyes glisten, ya walk jive, ya soul pop and ya love mighty ~ it is ever-changing ~ communal and individual ~ it is the paradox that you feel belies you ~ You have all this in you, and ya own special prism God has gifted you to emit it in~ You are black whether they tell you or not. Whether you think it or not. MAKE THEM LEARN TO LOVE IT MARS!

3.30

22 Elysium Gardens

Fantasia's house.

Arrived. Stopped outside.

It's a big house… Sheeeeett man.

Knock on the door, Mars.

> *He knocks and waits. And as the doors opens, a great white light appears.*

THREE

GOD: *(exclaiming the chorus of "Wookie's - Battle)* Everyday is like a battle , but we'll overcome. When we get back in the saddle, love will bring us home.

1. MARS

F.DAD: Yes?

MARS: You're white?

F.DAD: I beg your pardon?

MARS: I mean... I'm here for Fantasia. *(To Audience)* I feel my hands quake.

F.DAD: You mean Sia?

MARS: Sia, yeah – yeah.

F.DAD: OH Yes! Yes she told me she would be meeting someone today. Please do come in, she just ran to the shops. I'm her father.

MARS: Oh... thanks.

                     Fantasia... or Sia's... dad is an imposing figure. Tall like the money laundering sky scrapers he properly owns. He looked like he had grey , thundering rain clouds for hair and some fat pregnant stomach like he was about to give birth to a new, national recession.

F. DAD: So, you're the new one I'm guessing.

MARS: What you mean?

F. DAD: Her... protégé.

MARS: Don't you mean... boyfriend?

                     (To Audience) He laughs hard like he's about to die.

F. DAD: You are a good lad aren't you?

How much do you know about her? My friend, you thought her real name was Fantasia.

MARS: I know that she's very intelligent. Met her at the hospital I was staying at and she taught me all sorts of things. She has a thing about psychology right?

F. DAD: Indeed, a degree. Hospital did you say?

MARS: Yeah, um, had like likkle bouts of depression and that but like it's nothing. Really, everyone gets sad sometimes innit?

F. DAD: Yes. Mental Illness at such a young age though. You sure you're well enough for all this... march malarkey

MARS: Malarkey?

F. DAD: Would you like some tea.

MARS: Erm, yeah, feeling kinda parched still.

F. DAD: 2 sugars or 3?

MARS: Ehh just 2.

F. DAD: Have 3.

MARS: Ttthank yoou?

Trying to keep his quaking hand down, to Audience.

I wanna text her but my hand is moving vicious. But he ain't the one Prophet. He ain't done anything.

F. DAD: Sometimes it's hard for people to imagine Fantasia has a white dad. Especially in this day age which is frankly disconcerting.

I mean, don't get me wrong – I used to support BNP.

Sia is actually an orphan y'know.

MARS: Oh.

F. DAD: Refugee ~ Abandoned child from the 1990 Tuareg
           Rebellion in Mali ~ Buried desert marauders desperate to
           have their Timbuktu back from colonialization ~ I was a
           journalist covering the whole mess and the things I saw ~
           Son/ it was a Jammy Dodgers if you were white –

MARS: /Err I –

F. DAD: Everybody wants to talk about injustice here but THEY
           had it haaard since the 19th century.

           Gunshots lit the air and I dashed with my camera to a
           nearby well and – well… there she was. Guarding a
           mound of sand-washed bodies laced with the most ruby-
           red blood ~ It was like looking at melted hard candy if
           you can imagine it.

           Sia was a fighter. And when I looked into her eyes ~
           those incandescent eyes ~ she was so beautiful ~ Raw ~
           Sweet …she didn't deserve this. I had to save her.

           She swung a machete at me and shrieked
           'DIABLE'…Devil in French. Ha! Bless her. She was
           only 4. War was the only thing she knew... But that's
           over now, Right?

MARS: Well-

F. DAD: Y'know, personally, I don't see race.

           I just see a person…

           That I can fuck with ~ Sure you don't want some tea?

                    His hands suddenly shoots up towards the
                    machete in his backpack – he stops it just in
                    time.

MARS: NAH! Nah.

F. DAD: You alright son?

MARS: Don't... I think I need to go wash my face. It's been a
               long walk and feeling a little jittery, where's the toilet?

F. DAD: In your country upstairs to the right.

MARS: *(To Audience)* I go up the stairs and wash my face and—

               And washing his face.

               Am I the only one that's hearing it? Or is this you tryna
               mess with my mind Prophet?

               I can't kill her dad. It's her dad.

                       Looks to dry his hands and looks out the
                       window.

               I look outside and it's twilight. The way the sun is just
               balancing on the horizon like a don. And I see her from
               Machiavelli Park coming down the lane. And all the way
               from there she can spot me from the window. And she
               smiles this big smile. She is running for me! She's
               running.

               I hurry myself and go back downstairs

               Fantasia's dad is suddenly laid out all these papers on the
               floor

F. DAD: Photocopies of some of the case studies in her diary.
               You're interested in psychology, have a look at these.

MARS: Naaah that's bare intrusive.

F. DAD: Goooo oooooon son. Educate yourself on your woman.
               Know what she likes to talk about. Look at this one.

               Looks exactly like you.

               And this one.

And this one.

All past protégés may I add, and they really fell for her. Never she for them but – Oh there was one that she really loved.

Prophet he called himself, really cannot pronounce his real name. Did you see on the news how he was spectacularly slain by the police? The one she started all these dangerous march malarkey – turning against me for. And here comes... well, you.

The second chance.

So take your chance. Because women like her don't really stay around. I should know, I'm her dad.

Do you have one because if you did you would know how I feel right now you would know how I feel seeing someone like you tamper with this perfection I have created YOU make me SICK You feed off the benefits that we pay for like fools as if you're eating KFC or whatever deep-fried filth that you stuff into your gluttonous ungrateful mouth Acting like victims of a great society we have built that you will unfortunately lead Go Go home child Go home and bleed your mother dry Go to school and sit and the back of your class like the ignorant fool you are and staple your mouth shut Go back and drown in the grime of your estate Go get a knife and kill it's what you are good at but you see the thing is I know this is all lies I have always known I created them and you're a bit stronger than I thought you were and ooh you're moving a bit fast and you were not supposed to stay for so long you were not supposed to stay for so long you were supposed to come over here and slave not live and now I can't rid of you and I find I don't want to get rid of you because you guys have something, it seasons everything that you do and feeds my appetite but never fills me it's like this sweetness that's so Moorish it's like texture that's so gooey and I want it to be mine because I am white supremacist capitalist patriarchy I am racist Aryan greedy and sexist that bell hooks chick got it right and I really really can't let you go and I'm petrified of the powers you have because I know that if I forget myself all it takes is one fine day out of seven so I shall be the devil you pray against at night and with my white light I'll insidiously twist all your hopes and dreams into my submission and make you need me like I need you because your chocolate belongs to me dammit and I know that you can hear me I know that you can hear me

I know that you can hear me ~ but please continue to act like you don't want me to escort you guys there?

MARS: What did you just say?

F. DAD: I said are you sure don't want me to escort you guys to the march? You said you've walked such a long way.

MARS: No.

F. DAD: Oh okay. Anyway my princess is waiting for you. Have fun.

MARS: *(To Audience)* I go to walk down the stairs, arrive at the front door and see her

Her

My Goddess.

Who all of this was for.

SIA: Mars, sorry, I had to pick supplies.

You ready?

F. DAD: I just saying to your friend dear that I can drive you lot there –

SIA: No thanks dad.

F. DAD: It's really no bother –

SIA: I said no.

Merci.

Come on Mars.

MARS: As I leave, turn back to her Dad and very quickly say…

(To FANTASIA DADs) I heard you y'know

And, this man, he says plain as day.

F. DAD: What do you mean?

I didn't say anything.

2.   BOUNTY

BOUNTY: 1998

Bounty and Michelle had been invited to the inauguration of a new pirate Radio Station, funded by Prophet himself. They called it Pumplex FM.

How classy.

(To MICHELLE) If at any point you feel uncomfortable, just stay by me. These lot can get a bit frisky… especially with Sandra around.

MICHELLE: Don't worry. I'm excited! Really! Got myself a new dress and everything.

BOUNTY: *(To Audience)* Bounty and Michelle entered the lift, newly installed by the council with the new security camera burnt to a crisp, to the 14th floor.

The door opened and a waft of that a-grade bellowed out.

GOD: R-e-wind. Inter Selecta!

> *DJ performs a rousing announcement of the new station and then a thumping garage mix of 1997 onwards fills the house.*

BOUNTY: The place is thumping. Bomber jackets gang were jumping around the place like they were dodgems to the beat and 'bussin gun finga inna di rave'.

DJ: This for all the ladies out there feeling a likkle cold cos you mandem aint go no home training to warm yuh up!

MICHELLE: Wooooooooooooooooooooooooooooooooooooooo. Whaaaat. Whhhaaaaaat? Get out ma waay. This is dedicated to my bon bon!

BOUNTY: Sandra came bashing in and...

SANDRA: WOOOOOOOOOOOOOIIIII IS THAT BOUNTTTAAAAAAYYYYY

They share a live dance. For the first time, they are enjoying each other's company. And for a moment, there is something... They come in close.

Beat...

BOUNTY: Sandra, I can't... it would break her heart.

SANDRA: Yeah... I know... besides, you don't need me to do that.

BOUNTY: Wait. You never said that back then?

The DJ spins the record mightily and the whole scene goes plays like a record jammed – a chopped and screwed version of B15's 'Girls Like Us'.

BOUNTY: This don't feel right...

The DJ speaks...

DJ: Mandem, remember when DJ Pumplex said this yeah...

The DJ reveals herself as GOD.

GOD: One day you'll forget us. You'll forget me. You'll forget we were even there.

But we've always been there...

PROPHET enters, hobbling

BOUNTY: 'Hey Prophet!' Oh yes (*To PROPHET*) 'Hey.'

PROPHET: Huh? ...Oh yo. Yooo, you made it. Ugh...

BOUNTY: What is it?

PROPHET: Music's a little loud. Can you close the Balcony door?

BOUNTY: Yeah yeah that's cool.

            Bounty and Prophet stood on the balcony, overlooking
            the entire of London. So many tiny stars all plaited in a
            metallic sea of promise. Kingdom that nobody knows
            who really rules what.

PROPHET: You ever walk out of your hood and feel like there is
            something...sad happening here, but everybody's too
            scared to feel it.

            They gonna shut down the school.

BOUNTY: What?

PROPHET: You heard me baby. I hate white people. I hate—

BOUNTY: Hate is not your forte... Sorry

PROPHET: Hey... I can actually see a star out tonight.

            I have all the tools to build a rocket ship and fly to the
            stars. But, I can't leave you guys here. My family. No.
            Not just like that.

            It's lonely in space... ha!

            Well... not if you're with me.

BOUNTY: I've been thinking – we need to be more guerrilla with
            our education. Force it into the mainstream!

PROPHET: Begging again? Naa man. We need to do something
            bigger. Cut deeper. What your father did back then, was
            violent. But it was an act. A real act. So what I think we
            should do, is use the next Junkanoo as a call to arms. I
            can get connections. We can arm our people and we can
            split and storm two strongholds ~ The Obsidian Police
            Constabulary ~ which is just above the Iswandlwana
            Barbers ~ And the English National Front HQ. Now we
            don't know where that is – but that little cracker you used
            be friends with does. We've seen him and we know he'll
            talk to you. And y'know what we do when we get there...

            [We kill them]

                            Pause.

PROPHET: I would respectfully ask you not to look at me like that. /I already allowed you to raise your voice to me once.

BOUNTY: Prophet/Prophet I haven't even said anything.

PROPHET: Exactly. What?

BOUNTY: Prophet I can't. I can't kill.

PROPHET: You can't? Okay okay, maybe kill is the wrong word. See it as cleansing, we are cleansing our world of these parasites.

BOUNTY: Prophet, please there must be another way –

PROPHET: THERE IS NO OTHER WAY. DON'T YOU SEE NIGGA? I can't have children cos of them! Look at what they've done to me Bounty.

BOUNTY: Yes, yes sorry sorry –

PROPHET: No you ain't. No you ain't! Cos if you were you wouldn't be jittering like this! You think that cracker loves you? You think he loves you more than your own people?

BOUNTY: I know he's better and I know this is NOT the way forward.

PROPHET: What have I told you about raising your voice?

PROPHET: I will do whatever is necessary to free ma people ~ And you should too ~ You wanna be weak? You wanna be weak? You are WEAK if you let another person suffer for your mistake!

                    Pause

PROPHET: Bounty I-I-I'm sorry. I didn't mean it - BOUNTY

BOUNTY: /Michelle! /MICHELLE!/ Don't touch me.

                    MICHELLE enters.

MICHELLE: Babes, what's wrong? –

BOUNTY: We're leaving.

                    BOUNTY leaves the balcony to come back into the party without MICHELLE.

PROPHET: Ain't no need to make a scene! You will heed me.

BOUNTY: And so Bounty went to fetch his coat from the / other corner of ganja smashed room and heard Michelle say-

MICHELLE: I'M COMING BABES!

GOD: R-E-WIND

            GOD rewinds the scene in front of BOUNTY.

BOUNTY: *(To Audience)* Wait huh?

MICHELLE: Babes,what's wrong? –

BOUNTY: "We're leaving" Bounty said

            BOUNTY tries to move, but is chained to the scene.

BOUNTY: *(To GOD)* Wait...what's going on?

            Calling after BOUNTY as if he is already gone...

PROPHET: Ain't no need to make a scene! You will heed me.

MICHELLE: *(as BOUNTY is inside)* I'M COMING BABES.

            Prophet is it?

PROPHET: Err... yes ma'am

MICHELLE: With all due respect... please. Stop harassing Bounty.

PROPHET: Harassing? Is that what he told you.

MICHELLE: I know Bounty done and learn a lot from you. A-and it's great, I ain't black power or nuffin but it's really great. I can see where this leads. It always ends the same way, throughout history. /He's gonna be a dad.

PROPHET: /Queen. Empress. With all due respect, these are kingly matters. And if yo boy is gonna be a father maybe... maybe you could convince him to join/ the fight

MICHELLE: /He ain't fighting nuffin.

PROPHET: I raised him.

MICHELLE: And now me and my baby are stabilizing him. Be a good father and let us reap what you've sown –

            PROPHET swoops in and holds MICHELLE's bump.

PROPHET: Bitch I will decapitate yo nagging ass head and crush yo
            baby's skull to dust if it meant getting ma revenge.

MICHELLE: And there it is... the truth. Ain't bout us... it's all bout
            you. You couldn't even give a toss if he lived or died.

            Now, I'mma say this only once. Leave. Bounty. Alone.

            *MICHELLE leaves PROPHET and BOUNTY
            speechless.*

3.   MARS

MARS: 4pm

            The march is fulla people from all walks of life. All races
            all sexes.

            All chanting 'Black Lives Matter'.

            With that one that has to change it to 'All Lives Matter',
            so that they don't feel so left out.

            And watch my girl, Fantasia... Sia, walking like she one
            of them. Giving them testimonial diarrhoea to fuel their
            fantasies of a better world. She ain't even noticed I ain't
            said a word to her yet.

            Am I really just a project?

SIA: Take one of these. Balaclavas. You got the –

            MARS nearly pulls out the machete.

            NO. Not yet, not yet!

            But you did it though. I'm so proud of you! It's so good
            to see you!

MARS: We march down through Obsidian. Past Antebellum
            Bridge.

            SIA sings the chorus to "Battle" by Wookie.

MARS: Through Machiavelli Park. Past Aggro Estate. ~ Cutting
            through Isandwlana Road ~ Coffee shop after coffee shop
            after coffee shop ~ I'm going back on myself!

            My whole body is infested with Prophet's rage. Like
            every cell is desperately sealing back its own reservoir of

lava. It burns me so nicely. And with every step I feel the earth's core quake with me. Fam I can smell the impending pigs blood and it taste so good. Will drink it like wine with my Queen as we raise all this colonial shiit – NO

That's sick! That ain't me!

SIA:	Mars , we're here!
MARS:	It's the Obsidian Medical Centre… but also The Obsidian Police Constabulary. Hell.

The demons in blue start peering through their desk office windows.

SIA:	What do we want?
MARS:	Justice!
SIA:	When do we want it?
MARS:	Now!

Putting on the balaclava.

SIA:	What do we want?
MARS:	-
SIA:	What do we want?
MARS:	Blood.
SIA:	When do we want it?
MARS:	Now.
SIA:	What do we want?
MARS:	Your love.
SIA:	And when do we… wait, what?
MARS:	Fantasia… I like you. Like I really, really like you. You make me feel normal and… like extraordinary and messy at the same time.
SIA:	Oh Mars…
MARS:	Do you love me?

4. BOUNTY

BOUNTY:	1999. Bounty was 20. James Torbright aswshivering outside his flat on a cold July night.
	(To JAMES) Hey.
	JAMES nods.
	James had changed. Drastically. He looked at Bounty like... [meat]
	(To JAMES) I meant to buy some stuff from the shop today but I been busy with the Junkanoo.
	I'm lead organizer now. All we have is Michelle's chocolate if you want some –
JAMES:	You've changed.
BOUNTY:	What? How?
JAMES:	You're all... distant like. All knowledgeable and...
BOUNTY:	And what James?
JAMES:	-
BOUNTY:	James... you're not making any /sense.
JAMES:	I know, I know it's just... everything changing. The whole area is changing and like all this crime is going up and people getting shot and-and stabbed and... you know it's you lot. It's this black on black crime stuff. It is you lot killing each other and you know it Bounty. It's all over the news. Ain't I right?
BOUNTY:	Y-yeah but –
JAMES:	See... you ain't that smart huh? That's why you /left me right? Cos I'm dumb and /white and poor.
BOUNTY:	/What? /No. James I've never cared about that. And you know it.
	James, why you here? You've come all the way to my flat. What do you want?
JAMES:	FUCK OFF.
BOUNTY:	JAMES... Michelle and Moses are sleeping.
	JAMES curls up.

(Looks to JAMES) One black, hot, coal ring invading those baby blue eyes. *(To JAMES)* Hey, the room M&M are in is pretty sound proof though. You wanna listen to some low-level garage?

> *JAMES shrugs. BOUNTY plays some chill garage. MJ Cole's 'Sincere'. JAMES starts to nod his head.*

Ooh, so you like it.

JAMES :   No... it's you lot's music innit.

BOUNTY: 'You lot' James?

Is that why you're bobbing your head then?

> *BOUNTY catches JAMES' smile. Gets an ice pack.*

Let me see your eye. *(JAMES shows eye up close)* Gosh...

JAMES: Don't ask.

> *JAMES takes ice-pack. He risks sitting up close with BOUNTY. BOUNTY nurses him*

BOUNTY: Y'know the producer on this is white and the singer is black.

JAMES: NOOOOOO. I thought this was you people's kinda choon.

BOUNTY: I think it is...well born from us at least.

JAMES: Don't you mind? We always accused of stealing stuff. Don't you care?

BOUNTY: I do, but I don't mind as long as we are respected I guess-

JAMES: I'm sorry I said what I said 'bout your Dad, Bounty. That weren't on.

BOUNTY: No, it wasn't. But I'll accept your apology.

> *They sit in silence. BOUNTY stares at JAMES.*

JAMES: What?

BOUNTY: Nothing.

JAMES: Don't lie to me Bounty.

BOUNTY: James, I have missed you... but... I don't know why. I'm trying to remember all the good times and the laughter and the euphoria that I have had with you ~ but God has not taken me to any of them. I can't remember *any* of them. And those silent spaces in my story are screaming at me right now to jump out of the pool of your baby blue eyes before I drown. Once upon a time, you were the only thing I thought I had. I forgot them ~ I forgot Sandra & Michelle ~ I forgot they were even there ~ But they have always been there. But that's the beauty of retrospect. Does that make any sense James?

JAMES: You've missed me but...?

BOUNTY: Hmph. Nothing.

JAMES: Are you still my friend?

BOUNTY: Of course I am... but...

JAMES: But?

BOUNTY: James , I'm... I'm tired... of pretending –

JAMES: Pretending that you like me?

BOUNTY: No. But pretending that how... little you know bout me. About people like me... is okay.

            Do you understand?

JAMES: B-but... I know everything about you. You're my best friend...

BOUNTY: James... I know that like but... I'm tired of you wallowing in your own ignorance ~ Cos when you do that, people like me die. I'm gonna be a dad now and it's like I don't have time to skinteeth and –

JAMES: See what I mean??! You gone crazy? Why skinning your teeth for me. You're wearing away you a mammal for nuffin like.

                    Beat.

BOUNTY: WHY ARE YOU SO DUMB! *(To Audience)* Bounty though[t]-

JAMES: I knew you thought I was dumb.

BOUNTY: *(To Audience)* Did Bounty say that out loud? *(To JAMES)* Sorry… you're just so… uneducated.

JAMES: Well not anymore. I'm a knight now. Better than police. I'm an actual knight of the holy order. And you lot are dragons. Charring Britain to blackness. That's what my dad said. I'm part of crew and were gonna make Britain right.

> *Goes to leave but BOUNTY stops him. They scuffle and BOUNTY deliberately touches JAMES's scarred eye –*

OWWW!!

> *– at that moment MJ's Cole's Sincere track blends with a frantic drum and bass rhythm with an English football hooligan choir chanting 'who r ya'.*

JAMES: Let me go Bounty! I love you guys but you HATE me. I don't even get to go to your Junkenniny or whatever it is called cos you guys banned letting white people know where it is. Tell me *THAT* is not racist.

BOUNTY: It's to protect ourselves.

JAMES: Apart from that one time Bounty, I have never laid a finger on you.

BOUNTY: M-maybe not physically but mentally! We can't be racist! You guys profit from system daily

JAMES: REALLY? WHAT PART OF YOU FINKS THE SYSTEM WANTS ME?…What even the fuck is "the system" anyway?

BOUNTY: James…I'll…I'll tell you were the Jukenoo is.

JAMES: …Really? Bounty that's…big. But it ain't my place.

BOUNTY: How are we supposed to move forward if I let you stay like this. If you really love me, you will come.

JAMES: You know it ain't my place. I don't even know where it is –

JAMES: Ewwww you're gay. *(They share a brief moment of happier times)* Can I borrow this CD?

BOUNTY: Yeah let me go get it.

            BOUNTY exits the scene,

GOD: STOP.

            The shackles of GOD keep him watching.

            Enter MICHELLE, who had been sleeping.

MICHELLE: *(yawning)* Bounty what's all that... *(noticing JAMES)* Hi.

            JAMES watches her with deadly intent.

            Erm, you're James right? Bounty talks all about you. I'm Michelle –

JAMES: I know who you are. You're part of the pack. The pack that took him from me.

            They hold their stare and silence.

GOD: SLOW

            JAMES chants monkey noises at MICHELLE in slow motion. MICHELLE stands resilient.

MICHELLE: And there was me thinking you might have been as original and creative as Bounty. Shame.

GOD: PLAY.

            BOUNTY returns into the scene, angered.

BOUNTY: I got the whole CD and –

JAMES: Monkey head I don't want you to go –

BOUNTY: James! This is the kinda racist shit I mean.

JAMES: You would call me that?... The 'R' word?

BOUNTY: James, stop it. If you're coming to the Jukenoo, you're gonna need a leaflet

MICHELLE:	NO! You know the rules Bounty.
	AND He made Monkey noises at me.
BOUNTY:	Na you...you must've misheard right James?
JAMES:	You would believe her?
MICHELLE:	You don't believe me? /Bounty?
JAMES:	/...After all these years
BOUNTY:	"Like I said, you misheard. He would never knowingly do that. The system has twisted him, I can change that ~ I've known him longer than you" Bounty said
MICHELLE:	I can't believe...You and him have CHANGED. GROWN. Worlds apart. Stop trying to save him! We've talked about this!
BOUNTY:	"Really Michelle? In front of him?" Bounty said

Baby starts crying.

MICHELLE:	Ah! Bounty please, I really don't wanna talk about it anymore. Let your boy go.

MICHELLE goes.

BOUNTY:	"...I don't believe what she's saying " Bounty said...
	Bounty...I...I went to..to get a leaflet with all the details on it, including the address.
	'Come James. If you're truly not racist'
JAMES:	...Okay Bounty. I'll...I'll see you at the Junkanoo.

JAMES leaves.

BOUNTY:	*(To Audience)* Should've listened.

5. MARS

MARS:	Do you, love me?
SIA:	Mars, this is not the time. Put on your balaclava and take your machete.
MARS:	When will it be time Fantasia?
SIA:	What did you call me?

MARS: Fantas-

SIA: They're coming Mars, quick , quick.

MARS: *(To Audience)* The blue demons ooze out onto the
               pavement. The prophet hand pulls out the balaclava and –
               does she love me? – and reaches for the machete and—
               she doesn't love me and I reach for the hilt of the
               machete – and I don't think she…

SIA: You thought this was it.

               You thought a march will suffice

               Whilst you all salivate in your mosh pit

               And make blackness your sacrifice.

               But I don told you the vampire slayers are coming.

               And today's it's you who will bleed.

               With the grandson of Nana Ato Sackey

               Who will take the lead –

MARS: STOP RHYMING, IT'S DEAD

SIA: Huh?...Mars, I didn't even know I was rhyming.

MARS: *(To hand)* No Prophet. Not yet. Spirits hold him back!

               Do you like me?

SIA: Of course I do. Mars is this the time-

MARS: Do you love me?

SIA: Oh… Mars –

MARS: Could you love me?

               Could you at least try?

SIA: Mars… I don't see you like—

MARS: I should've listen to everyone when they said 'why would
               a girl like that want something to do with you?' All those
               time that you laid with me on the hospital green telling
               me you see something in me, saying that I could be
               anything I wanted to be/

SIA:	Which is true Mars/
MARS:	Oh don't bruv. Keep it. I'm a schoolyard project! I'm someone you finger yourself to with your little conscious bredrins at some chic bar with African drumming.
SIA:	Mars you are embarrassing us—
MARS:	Ohh, can't take one of your case studies exposing you and fakery, hm? Having a mental breakdown. You're studying psychology for fuck sake, deal with it.
SIA:	Mars….
MARS:	Your Dad—
SIA:	Has he been saying things that trigger you?
MARS:	A lotta things. In succession.
SIA:	I'm sorry, I shoulda warned you bout him. Now you know how hard I have it living there.

To SIA, who is trying to pull him to the side:

MARS:	NO Sia!
SIA:	No?
MARS:	The policemen start to chuckle. Let em laugh at this fakery.
SIA:	Mars, what're you doing?!
MARS:	What are *you* doing? Collecting all this info on me and boys like me? Can you imagine your Dad deliberately photocopied pages of your shit to show me what this all is really about. To look edgy.
	The crowd ooo.
SIA:	You both had no right!
MARS:	He had no right. I had no right. You had no right to lead me – but it's my fault. I let you and now here we are. In a middle of a march you don't even care about!
SIA:	What the hell do you mean!? I care! I – I'm the one that brought you here! Sorry I didn't mean to shout. Please, Mars. Mars. I do care about you. But you don't matter right now. They are LAUGHING at us.

MARS: I love you. You are my EVERYTHING like like all I have.

SIA: No, Mars.

This is not about you. I never asked you to love me. I never asked you to fetishize me or make me your new pin-up or poeticize me. All I ever wanted you to do is to believe in *you*.

Who the hell has time for love?

MARS: I ain't gonna do what you want. /You wanna (*the hand struggles*) You wanna make me a murderer for what you want.

SIA: /No. No Moses. Listen! Shh. This isn't murder, it is retribution. They're going back inside Prophet – I – I mean Mars please!

MARS: No but you mean Prophet. Ya mean Devonte, Ramone. Ya mean Ola, Kwaku, Ti-jean, Idrissa, Tunde, Bangora. Ya mean inner-city, intra-block, inside-black SECTIONED boys for just another 'feel sorry for the black yute' exercise innit? Cos if you do that – maybe you'll feel important. Maybe you'll feel black. Cos daddy don't make you feel like that.

SIA: Don't go there Mars.

MARS: NO. You're demon. Just like Prophet. You take something with good intentions and poison it! Let the crowd disapprove. You poison them too. I hope all the spirits tear you apart for being fucking hypocrite slave-master bitch and everyone knows, including daddy dearest-

SIA slaps MARS.

SIA: That is enough. You don't ever get to call me that. Mental or not.

Prophet took way too long, and so are you. Let me smash this fantasy you seem to live in.

The balance of time and space is disrupted as SIA smashes MARS' dreams.

What is doing a few two-step across graves of dead black boys and girls gonna do? Half the people in this place don't care about any of these people! Do you think any of dem man are actually listening? ~ They're just waiting for us to dance and sing and holler till they horny enough to suck each other off with their guiltiness ~ And with their new lubricated pricks they'll just rape us again ~ Of everything. They're just biding their time Mars~ with pawns like you and other men

Men who watch us screaming and do nothing~ Men who will love us and at the times we need them most, just leave ~ Or maltreat us and won't even show up to the fucking marches to just be there ~ And leave black girls out there washed white clean of faith ~ And yeah I am one of those girls cos you know the system will only ever see me as black. Even my Dad does.

I needed prove to them that there are black men out there who will stay and move with us.

And you will move with me. By any ~ means ~ necessary.

ONE DAY,

You will forget us!

You will forget me!

You will forget we was even there!

But we have always been there

Pouring the entire contents of the promised land

Into you...

So

Moses

take

Your

Machete

Mars...

AND ACT.

6. MARS & BOUNTY

BOUNTY: Summer 1999 and I…I..

GOD: Go on my boy. I'm wid you. Always.

BOUNTY: It was the first day that he took his son to the Obsidian Junkanoo.

He looked into his son's eyes and he saw so much hope, like

I was a superhero

And

It was a really nice day.

A really nice day…

And I was in the basketball court, just showing my son around.

And… and… th-th-there was the chocolate… this chocolate fountain Michelle had made. On her own stool. She was so proud of it, y'know. It was magnificent.

And Sandra came and she said

"Y'know what yeah? You make me sick Bounty. In like a sickly sweet kinda manner.

I'm slightly sloshed innit. But I'm proud of you innit. You shoulda been mine really but I guess ya girl and ya baby is nice innit. DON'T MESS THIS UP. Those that cannot hear must feel.

I woulda loved you y'know. I mean… really really loved you."

And Moses gurgled at his to be Godmother. She insisted on being that.

Prophet was there. Outside the cages. Just nods.

And I saw…James. He was trying to come in but the security wouldn't let him , This wasn't his place they said and I said 'I'm running this now and I want him to be here , let him through' and he just immediately ran to stay by the chocolate fountain

Everything was... Grayscale

I said James... 'It is so good to see you' And he said, ' I wish you weren't here.'

Something in my system moved vicious I said 'James?' and then he said 'Staaaaaaaaaaaayyyyy away.'

J-James looked straight at me. Like I did this.

James said to me 'Take your baby, take your girl and run'/ And James pulled out this... this phone. It weren't his usual phone. A-and e-everything moved in slow motion and Sandra started running towards me like she knew she knew she knew what was about to happen cos she must've seen the phone and for the first time in 12 years – I saw the baby blue of his eyes in full flow watering the barrenness, the gravel overlaying his face and with that sight I would truly like to believe he was sorry. And...

And it was because I could see him crying that I genuinely, stupidly thought I could get to him. I really did and I said 'James... why?'

And James just whispered...

'Run'

An explosion.

SIA/MICHELLE/SANDRA: AHHHHHHHHHHHHHHHHH!

BOUNTY: A nail bomb. Sounds of screams.

Skin being sliced

Children on fire.

The tinnitus in the ears after an explosion.

A nail, about 9 inches long

Drive straight through Sandra's right eye ~

And her chest

And her neck

And Michelle's tender womb

And one sliced just past Moses' cheek.

And suddenly there was no music.

Just the trickle of blood splattered around the estate.

By a racist.

Who used to be my friend.

And I looked to find this terrorist and he scattered like a rat and I looked to Prophet and in tears and he said:

ALL: So now what? What are you gonna do?

BOUNTY: And truth is...

MARS/BOUNTY: I don't know.

BOUNTY: I held Sandra in my arm as she cried, wailing for her mum – and felt like I was depriving her mum of this moment.   And I knew she was dying so I just... kinda cradled her as she went from queen-to-woman-to-girl-to-child – a new born baby –to-a-stillborn dream. And she closed her eyes and started to just... y'know... and all this promise melted in between my fingers.

And then she was gone.

And yet, Moses still looked at me like I could save him from this. Like I could be his hero.

That was the moment I realised I could never win. Not in this world.

THERE IS NO HOPE.

There is no hope. And that's why I left.

The sound of drip drops. PM enters.

MARS: I turn to the side and see...the Policeman from this Morning. He the only man in blue outside now.

MARS takes out the Machete. The sound of water running.

Fantasia. Fantasia. Fantasia. Fantasia. Fantasia.

MARS walks towards to BOUNTY, seeing him as the policeman. The sound of water is overflowing

Fantasia. Fantasia. Fantasia. Fantasia. Fantasia is a human being.

> *MARS gets right up to PM and brandishes the machete to his neck. The sounds of being submerged in water.*

It's like he wants me to. His troops are mobilizing inside by this act. And his tears I can see…him, swimming in the pools of sapphire.

But these spirits still flow with wrath through my body. And my hand needs to cut something.

> *MARS painfully takes the machete away from the PM's neck and slices into his own hand. The powerful scream of PROPHET bellows as he is being released from MARS' body.*

> *MARS takes his bloodied hand and smears it all the PM s face and right in his eyes. PM – understanding and distraught, exits.*

> *MARS walks back and hands SIA the machete.*

There's ya act.

SIA: Mars don't –

MARS: *MARS spiritually turns the sound of SIA's voice off.*

I walk I walk I walk I walk I walk I walk I walk I walk I walk I walk I walk I walk I walk I walk I walk I walk I walk

> *SIA – knowing she has failed – exits.*

> *MARS repeats this line underneath this section.*

> *SANDRA narrates the rest of BOUNTY's story.*

> *BOUNTY is made to play it out, his soul is dampened. His shackles ring. He is lifeless.*

SANDRA: The day it happened was December 31st 2000. 11:59. It was a millennium vigil.

You said to yourself Bounty, you can't be Michelle's lover Moses's dad. You couldn't protect them.

So, you put my Moses, who had sight of Mars in his eyes, back into Michelle's arms.

And she said…

'Where you going?'

BOUNTY: Nowhere, just need to get away… I'll be back soon.

MICHELLE: Okay Bounty. OKAY. But please… come back

BOUNTY: Yeah sure.

SANDRA;   You stood at the edge of Antebellum Bridge. Old and colonial and meretricious. You tried to breathe…

But you felt so wrong.

And before you knew you was no longer standing on the ledge of the bridge

And you just leaned forward. And just *(breathes)*

And you threw yourself over Antebellum Bridge.

SANDRA: *(To GOD)* Sorry Ms, I just know he can't.

GOD: And now, it's going to happen all over again.

BOUNTY: What?

GOD: Watch.

The light goes up on MARS.

MARS: To Antebellum bridge. And I look in the water.

SANDRA (who is the GIRL) appears.

BOUNTY: Is that? No stop it.

MARS: And I search for you Dad.

BOUNTY: *(To GOD)* STOP IT!! *(To SANDRA)* Sandra, tell her to stop it.

SANDRA: I can't! I can't meddle in the lives of humans no more. You need to come to him. You need to find a way to break through to him.

MARS: Sometimes it feels like I can't breathe. And today I don't want to.

BOUNTY:	I dunno what to do, I dunno what to do! I'm begging you please!
MARS:	You don't appear in my dreams, you don't travel into my memories. I forget what you look like. Mum keeps nothing of you.
BOUNTY:	I'M HERE SON! I'M HERE!
SANDRA:	He can't hear you or see you.

> *MARS begins to stand on the ledge of the bridge. He breathes.*

BOUNTY:	GOD PLEASE.
SANDRA:	How else does the dead contact the living?
BOUNTY:	errr… errr… d-dreams? DREAMS!
GOD:	Go after your son.
MARS:	I will find you.

> *MARS jumps.*

BOUNTY:	NOOOO
SANDRA:	Let him hit the water!
BOUNTY:	What the –
SANDRA:	Let him hit the water, he'll be unconscious. Soon as he lands, jump in and lock onto his scar. You won't have much time before he drowns!
BOUNTY:	Why are you helping me?
SANDRA:	Wai… What?
BOUNTY:	Sandra, I got you killed.
SANDRA:	This ain't that time, You need to get in there as soon as

> *MARS hits the water.*

BOUNTY:	I'm sorry Sandra.
SANDRA:	…That matter now, does it?
BOUNTY:	You don't forgive me/ do you?
SANDRA:	/He's nearly there Bounty, prepare yourself!

BOUNTY:	Let me burn and you save him ~ Or God save him ~ someone other than me
SANDRA:	NO! Stop doing this ~ Stop wallowing in your own, rassclart, stink!
	You have *no* idea what you have done and what you are /about to do.
BOUNTY:	/Yes I –
SANDRA:	LISTEN.

GOD pauses the world.

GOD:	It's time, let it out babygirl.
SANDRA:	Yes. I want to enjoy your pain. Yes, Your friend ~ your *best friend* ~ killed me. And I had dreams star. Plans. Destinies nobody's tiny mind in Obsidian could even think of. And I hate that yeah ~ And I hate it more because I know it's not your fault ~ your heart's just so big and now I can see just how hard it is to *see* ~ but there's something in us ~ given to us ~ to maybe not hear… but *feel* when it ain't right ~ and *feel* when it's time to act ~ and that's how I begged you to live ~ and you were so nearly there and sometimes I think I shoulda just dropped you like Michelle said you should drop that WATLESS DEMON and watch your entire bloodline fester , bend and spoil like mine did but for some...reason…I just can't.
	Cos… somewhere ~ to a girl like me ~ you are someone's Son, Father, Friend, Teacher, Brother, Love of their lives…and to watch you all fall ~ *incinerates* me.
BOUNTY:	…Sandra…I'm –
SANDRA:	BUT like I said, non-a-that matters now ~ YOU WILL BE THE ONE to save YOUR SON cos God knows ~ and I know ~ you can ~ SO ~ GO!

7. BOUNTY & MARS

MARS is submerged in water. He gains consciousness in this water. He finds he is able to walk through the water, as if it's just space. A white light starts to slowly envelope the stage. MARS walks towards the source of the light.

BOUNTY drops in and runs over and faces MARS for the first time. They are in awe of each other. BOUNTY opens his mouth but words do not flow out.

BOUNTY understands. BOUNTY touches MARS' scar that is under his eye with his thumb.

BOUNTY takes his left hand and plunges into MARS's chest. Straight through to his heart. We hear the voiceover mixing both BOUNTY and MICHELLE's voice together. This is the voiceover GOD is using.

EPILOGUE/OMEGA

Ω

A hospital room. MARS suddenly wakes up to see his mum peering over him.

MICHELLE: Moses!

MARS: Mum! Where ya been?

MICHELLE: I – I just needed a walk love – no, so selfish – forget about me. Are you okay?

MARS: No… I'm not.

MICHELLE: I'm sorry love. I'm so sorry I wasn't there ~

MARS: It's okay Mum. It's okay.

MICHELLE: Listen. It's not okay. I've been so sad after –

MARS: I know.

MICHELLE: I just needed some time… for me…

MARS: And me?

MICHELLE: …I should go.

MARS: NO! I can't –

MICHELLE: I have to tell them you're awake.

MARS: Oh.

MICHELLE gets up. Then…

He loved me, your dad.

And he *loved* you.

But your father didn't love himself. Normally. Extraordinarily. And in all the sweet mess. Even me I…

Find out what it means to love yourself Moses II.

And don't forget us.

Please, don't forget me. Don't forget that we are HERE. We always have been. And if you stay and if you rise up to the plate and you keep to your word, we will cook the promised land. And you and I will EAT ~ Just... eat... Do you understand?

MARS: Yes mum.

MICHELLE: I'll be back.

MICHELLE leaves.

MARS: Buyakasha.

The sun peers into my hospital window. It's a bit softer.

I'm still here.

And there it is,

that midsummer light.

Taking form and changing whatever it touches.

And the dead are soaring and passing through via the sunlight.

Wait...

A fantastical DJ remix of 'Sweet Like Chocolate, Boy' by Shanks and Bigfoot starts to play.

Via sunlight BOUNTY's spirit travels into the room.

GOD: I cannot give you much time. You got the length of a remix

He looks at his son for the first time. As a man

Honing into MARS' emotional scars, he touches them. They begin a fantastical lyrical dance through time.

Through times that could have been, should have and were. Through people, places and spaces. Through voices, speeches and roars

Through a blackness and whiteness

Through multicolour... Through OZ.

Through to the promised land

Together as a father and son. It is so... free.

> *And then, satisfied, BOUNTY crosses over and leaves.*

GOD: You are Sweeeeeeeeet like chocolate boy

Sweet like chocolate

GOD: You give me so much joy

You are

Sweet

Like Chocolate

Boy.

> *SANDRA appears- having earnt her wings – and sits by the foot of GOD*
>
> *MARS in a peaceful dream. MARS smiles and the water is gone.*

END OF PLAY

Illustrations

By Dan 'Old B' Christie

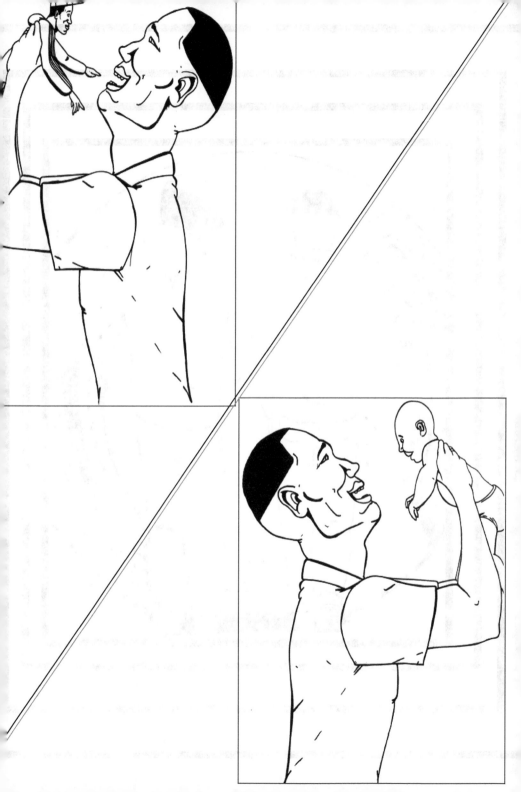

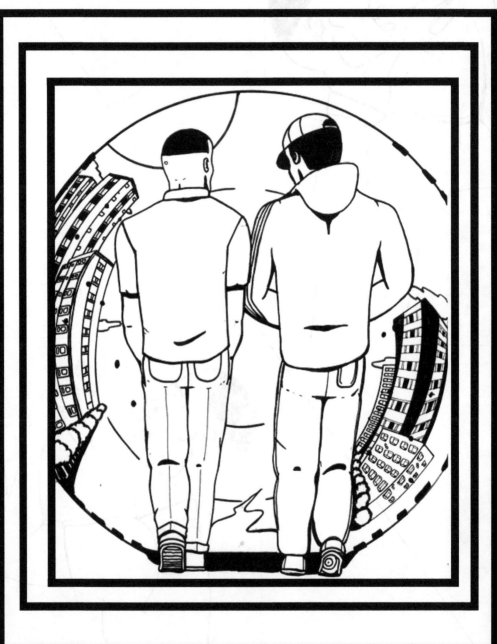

Sweet Like Chocolate Boy